Animal Welfare

Other Books in the Issues on Trial Series:

Animal Welfare

Sylvia Engdahl, Book Editor

GREENHAVEN PRESS
A part of Gale, Cengage Learning

Detroit • New York • San Francisco • New Haven, Conn • Waterville, Maine • London

Christine Nasso, *Publisher*
Elizabeth Des Chenes, *Managing Editor*

© 2010 Greenhaven Press, a part of Gale, Cengage Learning

For more information, contact:
Greenhaven Press
27500 Drake Rd.
Farmington Hills, MI 48331-3535
Or you can visit our Internet site at gale.cengage.com.

For product information and technology assistance, contact us at

Gale Customer Support, 1-800-877-4253
For permission to use material from this text or product, submit all requests online at www.cengage.com/permissions

Further permissions questions can be emailed to permissionrequest@cengage.com

Articles in Greenhaven Press anthologies are often edited for length to meet page requirements. In addition, original titles of these works are changed to clearly present the main thesis and to explicitly indicate the author's opinion. Every effort is made to ensure that Greenhaven Press accurately reflects the original intent of the authors. Every effort has been made to trace the owners of copyrighted material.

Cover photograph © David Cumming; Eye Ubiquitous/Documentary/Corbis.

LIBRARY OF CONGRESS CATALOGING-IN-PUBLICATION DATA

Animal welfare / Sylvia Engdahl, editor.
    p. cm. -- (Issues on trial)
    Includes bibliographical references and index.
    ISBN 978-0-7377-4737-9 (hardcover)
    1. Animal welfare--Juvenile literature. I. Engdahl, Sylvia.
    HV4708.A565 2010
    179'.3--dc22

                                                    2009039166

Printed in the United States of America
2 3 4 5 6 7 13 12 11 10

Contents

Chapter 2: Animals Cannot Be Named as Plaintiffs in Lawsuits

Chapter 3: Routine Farming Practices Are Subject to Anticruelty Regulations

Foreword

The U.S. courts have long served as a battleground for the most highly charged and contentious issues of the time. Divisive matters are often brought into the legal system by activists who feel strongly for their cause and demand an official resolution. Indeed, subjects that give rise to intense emotions or involve closely held religious or moral beliefs lay at the heart of the most polemical court rulings in history. One such case was *Brown v. Board of Education* (1954), which ended racial segregation in schools. Prior to *Brown*, the courts had held that blacks could be forced to use separate facilities as long as these facilities were equal to that of whites.

For years many groups had opposed segregation based on religious, moral, and legal grounds. Educators produced heartfelt testimony that segregated schooling greatly disadvantaged black children. They noted that in comparison to whites, blacks received a substandard education in deplorable conditions. Religious leaders such as Martin Luther King Jr. preached that the harsh treatment of blacks was immoral and unjust. Many involved in civil rights law, such as Thurgood Marshall, called for equal protection of all people under the law, as their study of the Constitution had indicated that segregation was illegal and un-American. Whatever their motivation for ending the practice, and despite the threats they received from segregationists, these ardent activists remained unwavering in their cause.

Those fighting against the integration of schools were mainly white southerners who did not believe that whites and blacks should intermingle. Blacks were subordinate to whites, they maintained, and society had to resist any attempt to break down strict color lines. Some white southerners charged that segregated schooling was *not* hindering blacks' education. For example, Virginia attorney general J. Lindsay Almond asserted, "With the help and the sympathy and the love and respect of the white people of the South, the colored man has risen under that educational process to a place of eminence and respect throughout the nation. It has served him well." So when the Supreme Court ruled against the segregationists in *Brown*, the South responded with vociferous cries of protest. Even government leaders criticized the decision. The governor of Arkansas, Orval Faubus, stated that he would not "be a party to any attempt to force acceptance of change to which the people are so overwhelmingly opposed." Indeed, resistance to integration was so great that when black students arrived at the formerly all-white Central High School in Arkansas, federal troops had to be dispatched to quell a threatening mob of protesters.

Nevertheless, the *Brown* decision was enforced and the South integrated its schools. In this instance, the Court, while not settling the issue to everyone's satisfaction, functioned as an instrument of progress by forcing a major social change. Historian David Halberstam observes that the *Brown* ruling "deprived segregationist practices of their moral legitimacy. . . . It was therefore perhaps the single most important moment of the decade, the moment that separated the old order from the new and helped create the tumultuous era just arriving." Considered one of the most important victories for civil rights, *Brown* paved the way for challenges to racial segregation in many areas, including on public buses and in restaurants.

In examining *Brown*, it becomes apparent that the courts play an influential role—and face an arduous challenge—in shaping the debate over emotionally charged social issues. Judges must balance competing interests, keeping in mind the high stakes and intense emotions on both sides. As exemplified by *Brown*, judicial decisions often upset the status quo and initiate significant changes in society. Greenhaven Press's Issues on Trial series captures the controversy surrounding influential court rulings and explores the social ramifications of such decisions from varying perspectives. Each anthology highlights one social issue—such as the death penalty, students' rights, or wartime civil liberties. Each volume then focuses on key historical and contemporary court cases that helped mold the issue as we know it today. The books include a compendium of primary sources—court rulings, dissents, and immediate reactions to the rulings—as well as secondary sources from experts in the field, people involved in the cases, legal analysts, and other commentators opining on the implications and legacy of the chosen cases. An annotated table of contents, an in-depth introduction, and prefaces that overview each case all provide context as readers delve into the topic at hand. To help students fully probe the subject, each volume contains book and periodical bibliographies, a comprehensive index, and a list of organizations to contact. With these features, the Issues on Trial series offers a well-rounded perspective on the courts' role in framing society's thorniest, most impassioned debates.

Introduction

During the past few decades public interest in the welfare of animals has been increasing. To be sure, deliberate cruelty to animals has been opposed for much longer than that, and most states have had laws against it since the nineteenth century. But in recent years stricter laws have been passed, and this trend is increasing. Furthermore, people have begun to be concerned about the routine treatment of animals—for instance, the condition of laboratory and farm animals.

Almost everyone agrees that animals should be treated humanely, but there are wide differences of opinion as to what practices are inhumane. Some people believe that it is sufficient to avoid the unnecessary infliction of pain on animals and provide them with adequate food, shelter, and health care. Others feel that it is cruel to confine animals in a way that prevents natural behavior. Still others, a vocal minority, maintain that animals should not be used by humans at all.

It is important not to confuse the animal welfare movement with the animal rights movement, although the two terms are often used interchangeably by people unfamiliar with them. Animal welfare advocates work toward the humane treatment of animals, but they do not object to most uses of animals for food, clothing, medical research, and other purposes that benefit humans, as long as these animals are well treated. Animal rights activists, on the other hand, oppose *all* human use of animals—even, in some cases, the ownership of pets.

A fundamental difference in philosophy separates these two movements. Animal welfare advocates believe that humans have a moral responsibility to ensure the well-being of animals. In contrast, advocates of animal rights hold that animals are the equals of humans and should have the same legal rights that people do. Some are very outspoken about this; for example, Peter Singer, in *Animal Liberation*—one of the earliest and best-known books on the subject—states, "Surely there will be some nonhuman animals whose lives, by any standards, are more valuable than the lives of some humans." This represents a view often stated by others. Moreover, where there is a conflict between human welfare and animal welfare, supporters of the rights movement tend to feel that the animals' interests have priority.

There is, of course, some middle ground. For instance, there are many vegetarians who believe it is wrong to eat meat yet do not equate animals with humans. There are many animal rights supporters who do not approve of the violent tactics, such as the bombing or burning of factory farms and research laboratories, in which the more militant activists engage. Critics, however, believe that the animal rights movement has damaged animal welfare efforts by arousing public antagonism.

Such antagonism has been engendered by not only violent incidents but also statements from animal rights activists that many people find offensive to minorities and often to the public in general. Animal rights activists have compared animal ownership to the former enslavement of African Americans. They have compared the killing of animals to the Holocaust in which the Nazis systematically murdered millions of people during World War II; Ingrid Newkirk, the cofounder of People for the Ethical Treatment of Animals (PETA), infamously said (as quoted in the *Washington Post* on November 13, 1983), "Six million Jews died in concentration camps, but six billion broiler chickens will die this year in slaughterhouses." The public was outraged by this trivialization of human suffering and by PETA's later "Holocaust on Your Plate" advertising campaign, in which pictures of people dying in concentration camps were displayed next to pictures of chickens and pigs.

Realizing that tactics of this kind will never win broad public support for animal rights, some groups within that movement have joined forces with animal welfare advocates in pushing for laws requiring better treatment of animals. Some observers feel that this is merely an attempt on the part of rights advocates to subtly promote their own agenda by calling attention to the mistreatment of animals. Animal owners maintain that such mistreatment is not as widespread as their opponents claim and that the real progress that has been made toward improving the condition of animals is often downplayed.

Surprisingly, there are animal rights activists who oppose animal welfare laws. For example, Gary Francione, the codirector of the Rutgers University Animal Rights Law Center, stated in the January/February 1992 issue of *The Animals' Agenda*, "Not only are the philosophies of animal rights and animal welfare separated by irreconcilable differences ... the enactment of animal welfare reforms actually impedes the achievement of animal rights. Welfare reforms, by their very nature, can only serve to retard the pace at which animal rights goals are achieved." These activists feel that if people believe animals are protected by laws, they will be less likely to say humans should not be allowed to own them.

There are two areas in which significant reform has taken place. The first is in the treatment of animals used for medical research. The federal Animal Welfare Act of 1970 and its subsequent amendments set rules for the procurement and care of these animals, and much more consideration is now given to their psychological needs than in the past. In addition, many scientists now adhere to what are known as the Three Rs—Replacement, Reduction, and Refinement. This means that wherever possible, researchers *replace* animal experiments with other techniques, such as computer modeling. Where the use of animals is necessary, they strive to *reduce* the number required through better design of experiments. Finally, they *refine* experimental procedures and animal living conditions to minimize distress—for example, by providing "enriched" cages with toys, hiding places, and nesting materials.

The other area coming under increased scrutiny is the treatment of farm animals. As discussed in chapter 3 of the current volume, some of the conditions under which these animals live, and some of the procedures commonly involved in raising them, are now viewed by many people as inhumane. This is a controversial issue, because practices that may seem cruel to observers are not considered cruel by farmers and veterinarians, who assert that these practices are often designed to prevent worse conditions from occurring. Also, while there are some farmers who give little consideration to the well-being of their animals, there are many others who make every effort to keep them healthy. Recently there has been an effort to legislate bans on some routine agricultural practices such as the keeping of laying hens in battery cages where they have little room to move; in some states these are succeeding.

Yet another controversial issue is the use of animals in zoos and circuses. Some people believe that there should be no zoos. They maintain that for animals to be confined is unnatural and detrimental to the animals' mental and physical health. Moreover, they contend, viewing live animals in zoos is not necessary now that videos of animals in the wild are accessible to everyone. Others argue that animals in large, well-maintained zoos are better off than they would be if exposed to the dangers of the wild and that those born in captivity are content. Zoo supporters point out that although the animals cannot roam over long distances, as they would in their natural habitat, they do not need to because they do not need to forage for food.

A lawsuit against Ringling Brothers and Barnum & Bailey Circus over the alleged mistreatment of circus elephants, which has been pending for many years, was finally heard by a federal court early in 2009. A coalition of animal protection organizations claimed that the elephants are chained for long periods and forced to perform through the use of bullhooks, causing them pain. This, they argued, is a violation of the Endangered Species Act, although that law has never before been applied to captive animals. Ringling Brothers maintains that its elephants are not treated cruelly and that if it is prohibited from using chains and bullhooks, elephants can no longer appear in the circus—a result that animal rights activists would welcome. As this book goes to press, the court has not yet made its decision. However, advocates for elephants feel that the publicity surrounding the case has already resulted in a significant change in public attitudes toward circus animals.

CHAPTER 1

Animal Welfare Advocates Take a Cruelty Case to the Supreme Court

Case Overview

Primate Protection League v. Tulane Educational Fund (1991)

The case of the Silver Spring monkeys is one of the best-known and most significant animal welfare cases in the history of the United States, perhaps the world. It is significant in a number of ways. It was the first such case to be fought all the way to the U.S. Supreme Court, and it created new public concern about the treatment of laboratory animals. It was instrumental in the establishment of People for the Ethical Treatment of Animals (PETA), a radical organization that has become a leader in the animal rights movement. It resulted in new knowledge about how best to care for animals used in research. Finally, it led to the discovery of important information about the brain that not only is of benefit to stroke victims, but also—as has been recognized fairly recently—represents a revolutionary new understanding of how humans' abilities develop throughout their lives.

The monkeys belonged to the Institute for Behavioral Research (IBR) in Silver Spring, Maryland. Edward Taub, the chief research scientist at IBR, had received a grant from the National Institutes of Health (NIH) to study somatosensory deafferentation, which means the surgical severing of sensory nerves so as to eliminate sensation in limbs. Although an animal (or a person) normally loses the use of a limb that has no feeling even if its motor nerves remain intact, Taub believed that sensory feedback is not essential to movement. He wanted to prove this by forcing the monkeys to use arms that had been deafferentated. He knew that if the monkeys could do this, stroke victims could, too.

Alex Pacheco, a college student, offered to serve as a volunteer in Taub's lab. He did not tell Taub that he was a cofounder of PETA working undercover to expose animal abuse. Pacheco reported finding appalling conditions in the lab, including not only filth and lack of humane care but also actual torture of the monkeys. While Taub was away, Pacheco took photos and called in scientists known to be sympathetic to PETA's cause to corroborate his statements. He then went to the police, who raided the lab and charged Taub with cruelty to animals. Though he was found guilty by a judge, Taub was entitled to a jury trial, at which his lawyers claimed that the caretakers hired for the monkeys had been bribed to stay away. He also explained that the monkeys' injuries had been self-inflicted because they could not feel pain in their deafferentated arms. Ultimately, he was convicted only on the charge of failing to provide veterinary care, and when he appealed, his conviction was overturned on the grounds that federally funded researchers were not subject to state laws. During the next few years Taub was also exonerated by several scientific organizations that had at first opposed him, although it took much longer for him to regain his reputation.

Meanwhile, there had been a long series of battles over custody of the monkeys. When first seized by the police in 1981, they had been turned over to PETA because there was no room for them in the zoo. Taub had obtained an injunction ordering their return, but they "mysteriously" disappeared and were returned only when it became apparent they were needed for evidence against him. Back at IBR, one of the monkeys died, whereupon the judge ordered them taken to an NIH quarantine center in Maryland. But PETA, now joined by the International Primate Protection League (IPPL), wanted them sent to a wildlife sanctuary in Texas, and the organizations lobbied Congress until, in 1986, members of the House of Representatives signed a petition requesting that this be done. However, the NIH sent the monkeys instead to the Delta Regional Primate Research Center in Louisiana, which was run by Tulane University. The next year it was persuaded by members of Congress to send some of the monkeys to the San Diego Zoo in California, but the rest remained at Delta. In 1984 PETA and IPPL filed a lawsuit requesting that they be named legal guardians of the monkeys, but it was dismissed on the grounds that they did not have legal standing to file the suit. The court of appeals upheld this ruling, and in 1987 the Supreme Court declined to review the case.

NIH had promised that no more experiments would be done on the monkeys. However, when the remaining ones were in such bad shape that it was felt they should be euthanized to spare them further suffering, NIH proposed a new project. Neuroscience had been advancing since Taub's original studies, and scientists now suspected that the brain—which had been thought not to change in adults—might be altered by the effects of damage to the body. The Silver Spring monkeys' brains had been without sensory input from their arms for more than ten years, far longer than any other experimental animals. Could their brains have changed in that time so that the area previously used to sense arms was used for something else? NIH decided that while the monkeys were anesthetized prior to euthanasia, their brains would be examined to see if this was true. Congress and the public, however, were angry about this plan. Even though the monkeys would not be conscious and would not feel anything, it seemed a violation of the promise NIH had made.

IPPL and PETA filed another suit, this time in a Louisiana state court, to prevent the euthanasia of the monkeys. The court issued a restraining order, whereupon NIH removed the case to federal court, which under certain circumstances federal defendants are allowed to do. The U.S. Court of Appeals for the Ninth Circuit ruled that the organizations did not have standing to sue for custody of the monkeys, but IPPL and PETA protested that for legal reasons, the case should not have been moved to federal court, and the Supreme Court agreed to resolve this question. This was the first time a case involving laboratory animals had reached the Supreme Court, and for that reason it is significant in the history of animal welfare litigation. The Supreme Court, however, did not make any decisions about the monkeys' fate. It merely said that even if the animal welfare organizations lacked standing to sue for the monkeys, they did have standing to sue for the right to be heard by the state court, and in 1991 the Court ruled in their favor by sending the case back to the Louisiana court. By this time the monkeys were already dead, but the timing made no difference since the Louisiana court also ruled that IPPL and PETA had no standing to sue.

What no one realized until much later was that the experiment done at the time of the monkeys' euthanasia resulted in one of the most important discoveries ever made about the brain. As Jeffrey M. Schwartz and Sharon Begley state in their 2002 book *The Mind and the Brain: Neuroplasticity and the Power of Mental Force*, "The Silver Spring monkeys . . . changed forever the dogma that the adult primate brain has lost the plasticity of childhood." This knowledge has led to a new therapy, developed by Taub, that is helping thousands of stroke victims to regain use of paralyzed limbs. But more than that, it has overturned the former belief that an individual's potential is determined entirely by genes and that adult brains cannot develop capabilities beyond those they originally had. The science of neuroplasticity is likely to transform the treatment of many conditions, mental as well as physical, and some believe it means that people can change their own brains by how they choose to think.

If the outcome of *Primate Protection League v. Tulane Educational Fund* had been different—if the animal rights organizations had been granted standing and had succeeded in preventing the monkeys from being euthanized—these discoveries would have perhaps been delayed for many years (and even then would have required experimentation on other animals). Some people think animals should not be used for research even when the well-being of large numbers of humans is at stake. Others think that although lab animals should never be mistreated as the Silver Spring monkeys had been, knowledge that benefits human beings is worth using animals to obtain.

> *"Petitioners' injury is clear, for they have lost the right to sue in Louisiana court—the forum of their choice."*

Unanimous Opinion: Animal Welfare Advocates Have the Right to Sue in the Court of Their Choice

Thurgood Marshall

Thurgood Marshall was the first African American to serve as a justice of the Supreme Court. He wrote the following opinion in Primate Protection League v. Tulane Educational Fund, *which represents the Court's unanimous decision. This was the culmination of a long series of cases in which animal welfare advocates tried to prevent further experimentation on a group of monkeys known as the Silver Spring monkeys. Repeatedly, courts ruled that the advocates lacked standing—that is, did not have the right to sue on behalf of the monkeys—because the advocates were not their owners and had suffered no personal injury in connection with them. The case is famous in part because it was the first case involving laboratory animals to reach the Supreme Court; however, the Court did not consider the fate of the monkeys, but only whether the National Institutes of Health had the right to move the case from state court to federal court, which it had done because the state court had issued a temporary restraining order preventing it from euthanizing the monkeys. As Marshall explains, although the petitioners themselves did not suffer any injury from treatment of the monkeys, they were in-*

Thurgood Marshall, unanimous opinion, *Primate Protection League v. Tulane Educational Fund*, U.S. Supreme Court, May 20, 1991.

jured in the legal sense by not being allowed to sue in the court they had chosen. Therefore, the Supreme Court ruled that the case must be remanded to the state court.

This case arose from an animal welfare dispute. At issue is the fate of certain monkeys used for medical experiments funded by the Federal Government. The case comes before us, however, on a narrow jurisdictional question: whether a suit filed in state court challenging the treatment of these monkeys· was properly removed to the federal court by respondent National Institutes of Health (NIH), one of the defendants. We hold that removal was improper and that the case should be remanded to state court.

Petitioners, who are organizations and individuals seeking the humane treatment of animals, filed this suit in Louisiana civil district court; the monkeys are housed at a primate research center in that State. Three defendants were named and are respondents here. Respondent Institutes for Behavior Resources (IBR) is a private entity that owns the monkeys. Respondent NIH now maintains custody of the monkeys, with IBR's consent. Respondent Administrators of the Tulane Educational Fund (Tulane) is the governing body for the primate research center that, in 1986, entered into an agreement with NIH to care for the monkeys. The suit sought to enjoin further experimentation on the monkeys and to obtain custody over them. Petitioners based their claim for this relief upon Louisiana law, including provisions that (1) impose criminal sanctions for cruelty to animals, (2) permit officers of humane societies to remove, to a "stable," animals being subjected to cruelty or that are "bruised, wounded, crippled, abrased, sick, or diseased," (3) authorize tort damages for "[e]very act whatever of man that causes damage to another," and (4) direct courts to "proceed according to equity" in situations not covered by "legislation or custom."

Shortly after the suit was filed, NIH removed the case to federal court pursuant to [a law], which authorizes removal of state suits by certain federal defendants. The federal District Court then granted a temporary restraining order barring NIH from carrying out its announced plan to euthanize three of the remaining monkeys and, in the process, to complete some of the medical research by performing surgical procedures. . . .

On appeal, NIH argued, *inter alia* [among other things], that petitioners were not entitled to the injunction because they lacked standing to seek protection of the monkeys. Petitioners, in turn, argued that the District Court had no jurisdiction over the case because [the law] permits only federal officials—not federal agencies such as NIH—to remove cases in which they are named as defendants. The Court of Appeals for the Fifth Circuit agreed with NIH that petitioners could not satisfy the requirements under Article III of the United States Constitution for standing. It also held that federal agencies have the power to remove cases. Accordingly, the Court of Appeals vacated the injunction and dismissed the case. We granted certiorari [review] to resolve a conflict between the Courts of Appeals for the Fifth and Third Circuits on the question whether [the law] permits removal by federal agencies. We conclude that it does not.

A Right to Sue in State Court

We confront at the outset an objection raised by NIH to our jurisdiction over the removal question. NIH argues that, because the Court of Appeals found that petitioners lack Article III standing to seek protection of the monkeys, petitioners also lack standing even to contest the removal of their suit. We believe NIH misconceives both standing doctrine and the scope of the lower court's standing ruling.

Standing does not refer simply to a party's capacity to appear in court. Rather, standing is gauged by the specific common-law, statutory or constitutional claims that a party presents. . . .

It is well established that a party may challenge a violation of federal statute in federal court if it has suffered "injury that fairly can be traced to the challenged action of the defendant," *Simon v. Eastern Kentucky Welfare Rights Org.*, and that is "likely to be redressed by the requested relief." *Allen v. Wright.* In the case now before us, petitioners challenge NIH's conduct. Petitioners' injury is clear, for they have lost the right to sue in Louisiana court—the forum of their choice. This injury "fairly can be traced to the challenged action of defendants," since it directly results from NIH's removal of the case. And the injury is "likely to be redressed" if petitioners prevail on their claim because, if removal is found to have been improper under [the law], the federal courts will lose subject matter jurisdiction and the "case shall be remanded." Therefore, petitioners clearly have standing to challenge the removal.

Nothing in the Court of Appeals' decision undermines this conclusion. The court below found that petitioners did not have standing to protest "disruption of their personal relationships with the monkeys," to claim "harm to their 'aesthetic, conservational and environmental interests,'" or to act as advocates for the monkeys' interests. But at no point did the Court of Appeals suggest that petitioners' lack of standing to bring these claims interfered with their right to challenge removal. Indeed, it was only *after* the court rejected petitioners' standing to protect the monkeys that it considered the question whether NIH's removal was proper. NIH argues that, were we also to consider the propriety of removal, "the Court would be resolving the removal question in a context in which the court below specifically found the injury in fact necessary to [the concrete] adverseness [required for standing] to be lacking." We disagree. The "adverseness" necessary to resolving the *removal* question is supplied not by petitioners' claims for the monkeys' protection but rather by petitioners' desire to prosecute their claims in state court.

"An interest in humane treatment of
animals is not enough to establish
standing [to sue] in the absence of a
link to the particular animals at issue."

Animal Welfare Advocates Lack Standing to Take Animal Mistreatment Issues to Court

Kenneth Starr

At the time of this case Kenneth Starr was the U.S. solicitor general; that is, the chief government attorney who argues before the Supreme Court when the federal government is party to a case. In the following brief for the National Institutes of Health, which is a federal agency, he argues that the Supreme Court should not grant review of the lower court's decision in Primate Protection League v. Tulane Educational Fund. *In this case, animal welfare advocates sued to prevent the euthanizing of the so-called Silver Spring monkeys, which they believed had been mistreated while being used for research. The lower court had ruled that the advocates had no standing to sue because they had not personally suffered any harm. Although the advocates claimed a personal relationship with the monkeys, this relationship resulted mainly from the suit and would not continue even if the monkeys were not euthanized, as the monkeys were privately owned. Moreover, the court had ruled that being troubled by the inhumane treatment of animals is not a personal injury entitling anyone to sue. In Starr's opinion, this decision was correct according to the legal precedents. Also, he argues, under the Constitution a state*

Kenneth Starr, brief for the National Institutes of Health, *Primate Protection League v. Tulane Educational Fund*, September 1990.

law—in this case the law against cruelty to animals—cannot be used to regulate the federal government's actions.

This case concerns the care and custody of macaque monkeys that were the subject of experiments to discern whether the monkeys recovered use of limbs after nerves to the limbs were severed. The experiments were conducted during 1981 by a private research facility—then called the "Institute for Behavioral Research, Inc.," later the "Institutes for Behavior Resources" (IBR)—under funding from the National Institutes of Health (NIH). The purpose of the experiments was to gain information that could be used in rehabilitating human patients with neurological damage.

In September 1981, Maryland police executed a warrant at IBR and seized the monkeys, acting upon allegations that the monkeys were being mistreated. Pursuant to a court order, NIH assumed custody of the monkeys. After that order expired, NIH continued to act as the monkeys' principal custodian with the consent and cooperation of the monkeys' owner, IBR.

In December 1988, NIH announced plans to perform euthanasia on three of the monkeys pursuant to the recommendation of a panel of independent experts. These three monkeys were then being kept at Tulane University's Delta Regional Primate Research Center. The euthanasia procedure, which would involve deep surgical anaesthesia, was designed to be humane and painless and to gain knowledge that could lead to improvements in rehabilitation therapy for persons who have suffered brain or spinal cord damage, a stroke, or similar injuries.

Before NIH could carry out the euthanasia, petitioners sued NIH, IBR, and the Administrators of Tulane Educational Fund (Tulane) in Louisiana state court. Petitioners sought an order enjoining the euthanasia and granting custody of the monkeys to petitioners or members of the U.S. Congress. After the state court granted petitioners' motion for a temporary injunction barring respondents from performing euthanasia on the three monkeys, NIH removed the case to the United States District Court for the Eastern District of Louisiana. NIH then moved to dismiss the case on, among other grounds, petitioners' failure to establish Article III [of the U.S. Constitution] standing to sue. . . .

Petitioners Suffered No Harm

The court of appeals agreed that none of the three bases for standing alleged by petitioners satisfied Article III requirements; it accordingly vacated the injunction and dismissed the case. With regard to the first basis asserted—a "permanent disruption of (petitioners') personal relationships with the monkeys"—the court observed that the Fourth Circuit had already rejected the "virtually identical" claim when in previous litigation the claim was asserted against IBR by two of the petitioners herein. The court below adopted the reasoning of the Fourth Circuit, which held that petitioners had not established a sufficient causal connection between the alleged injury and the conduct complained of: "(E)ven if the defendants were to comply with the laws putatively violated, the plaintiffs would still lack any right to continue their personal relationships with the monkeys." The court below further held that petitioners' second and third allegations of Article III injury— asserting harm to their "long-standing, sincere commitment to preventing inhumane treatment of animals" and to their "mission as advocates for the rights" of the monkeys—did not state cognizable injuries. For this holding, the court below relied principally on *Sierra Club v. Morton*, and *Valley Forge Christian College v. Americans United for Separation of Church and State*.

The court of appeals also held that the case was properly removed. Relying on prior decisions of the Fifth Circuit, the court rejected petitioners' argument that [the law] does not authorize removal by federal agencies. The court also rejected petitioners' argument that, although they had named NIH as a defendant, NIH's interest in the monkeys was insufficient to permit removal. The court concluded that "the only prerequisite to removal of a civil action is that it be brought against a federal officer or agency." The court further concluded that "NIH's possessory, financial and research interests" in the monkeys were sufficient to warrant the protection of a federal forum afforded by the removal statute.

After the court of appeals issued its ruling and denied petitioners' motion for a stay of mandate pending certiorari [review by the Supreme Court], respondents performed the euthanasia procedure previously planned for three of the monkeys. Earlier, upon the court's granting petitioners' motion for partial immediate resolution of the appeal, NIH had also performed euthanasia on a fourth monkey that was in severe pain and danger of imminent death. The case is not moot, however, because four monkeys of the original group of seventeen are still alive and are being housed at the Delta Regional Primate Research Center in Louisiana.

Unrelated Injury

The decision of the court of appeals is correct and presents no issue meriting review by this Court.

1. The court of appeals' ruling that petitioners' pleadings did not establish Article III standing is correct and does not conflict with any decision of this Court or any court of appeals.

Petitioners' complaint alleged three forms of injury: (1) "permanent disruption of their personal relationships with the monkeys," (2) impairment of their "sincere commitment to preventing inhumane treatment of animals, especially as concerns the monkeys now at Delta," and (3) impairment of their "mission as advocates for the right of the Silver Spring Monkeys, who have no means of protecting themselves." None of these allegations demonstrates Article III standing.

a. Petitioners' first allegation of injury was addressed by the Fourth Circuit in a case that this Court declined to review. *International Primate Protection League, Inc. v. Institute for Behavioral Research, Inc. (IPPL)*. In *IPPL*, two of the petitioners in this case alleged that the same conduct complained of here caused "disruption of their personal relationship" with the same group of monkeys involved in this case. The Fourth Circuit held that these allegations did not demonstrate standing because the asserted injury was not fairly traceable to the challenged conduct: "(T)hese plaintiffs could not see the monkeys in the IBR laboratory if the defendants satisfied all requirements of care." Petitioners now concede that this holding was correct.

The holding denying standing in *IPPL* is fully applicable in this case, as the court below recognized. Here, as in *IPPL*, any relationship between petitioners and the monkeys has come about largely in the course of litigation. To this extent, any disruption flows from the vicissitudes of litigation and is not cognizable injury in fact. Any other ties that may exist are jeopardized, not by the conduct complained of, but by the fact that these monkeys are privately owned research animals. It is the fact of private ownership, about which petitioners do not and could not complain, that causes the alleged injury. In short, petitioners' assertion of a "right of future contact" with the monkeys suffers from the same "traceability" defect identified in *IPPL*.

Petitioners cannot cure this defect by asserting that they sought broader relief in this case than they did in *IPPL*. . . . Petitioners thus offer no reason why the Fourth Circuit's admittedly correct ruling in IPPL should not apply here.

This is not to say that petitioners fare any better in satisfying Article III's requirement that they show their alleged injury "is likely to be redressed by a favorable decision." *Simon v. Eastern Kentucky Welfare Rights Organization.* On the contrary, as the court below held—a holding that petitioners do not challenge—petitioners' complaint failed to allege that they had met the statutory prerequisites to removal of the primates from NIH's custody under Louisiana law. This failure, as the court below correctly observed, distinguishes this case from those in which plaintiffs have included officials authorized by state law to prosecute violations of animal cruelty laws. Moreover, none of petitioners' other state law causes of action entitled them to continue their relationships with the monkeys or to be granted custody of them.

State Law Cannot Regulate Federal Conduct

b. The court of appeals was correct when it held that plaintiffs' second and third allegations of injury were insufficient to create Article III standing. In *Sierra Club*, this Court addressed an allegation substantially similar to petitioners' second allegation, which asserts a long-standing commitment to preventing inhumane treatment of animals. The Court concluded that assertion of such an interest does not satisfy the "require(ment) that the party seeking review be himself among the injured." Just as an interest in conservation was not enough in *Sierra Club* to establish standing in the absence of a link to the particular lands at issue, so too here an interest in humane treatment of animals is not enough to establish standing in the absence of a link to the particular animals at issue here.

In *Valley Forge*, the Court addressed an allegation substantially similar to plaintiffs' third allegation, which asserts their role as advocates for the primates. The Court in *Valley Forge* expressly rejected the notion that standing should be granted simply because judicial review otherwise would be unavailable. The court of appeals' application of *Sierra Club* and *Valley Forge* to conclude that petitioners' second and third allegations of injury were insufficient was clearly correct.

c. In any event, the court of appeals would have been justified to dismiss this case on Supremacy Clause grounds. The Supremacy Clause [of the U.S. Constitution] plainly bars petitioners' attempt to use the state law causes of action alleged in their complaint to regulate the federal government's custody of the monkeys. The Supremacy Clause required dismissal of the private defendants as well as NIH in this action, because the state law causes of action petitioners asserted would have effectively prohibited NIH from carrying out its plans to perform euthanasia on the monkeys. So applied, state law would directly conflict with the federal policy against interference with federally funded research that employs laboratory animals.

"The idea that animals should be protected if and only if a human being is adversely affected is antiquated, inhumane, and out of step with reality."

Courts Should View Animals as More than Mere Personal Property

Lauren Magnotti

At the time this article was written, Lauren Magnotti was a student at St. John's University School of Law in New York. In it she explains the legal principle of standing, under which only persons who have been harmed are allowed to initiate lawsuits. This prevents defenders of animal welfare from suing to stop the abuse of animals, since only the animal, not the person, has suffered injury. Animal owners can sue for injury to their property, but often it is the owner who is the abuser. For example, in Primate Protection League v. Tulane Educational Fund, *monkeys used for research were mistreated in the laboratory run by their owner, and courts ruled that animal rights advocates did not have standing to sue. Magnotti says that such cases show that the current system does not work. She argues that courts should treat animals as something more than property and that people other than the animals's owners should be allowed to sue on the animals' behalf.*

Lauren Magnotti, "Pawing Open the Courthouse Door: Why Animals' Interests Should Matter When Courts Grant Standing," *St. John's Law Review*, vol. 80, Winter 2006, pp. 465–74, 478–82, 494–95. Copyright © 2006 St. John's Law Review. Reproduced by permission.

In order to bring any suit, one must have standing. Animals are legally categorized as property and, therefore, are viewed as legal things and not legal persons. . . . Thus, since animals have no legal personhood and, as a result, no legally enforceable rights, they typically cannot bring suit on their own behalf. Consequently, it is left to individuals and organizations working on behalf of animals to bring suit when animals need protection. Because those bringing suit have generally not experienced an obvious injury in fact, their cases are often dismissed for a lack of standing.

It is well established that for a party to have standing, she must demonstrate that she has suffered an injury in fact, that her injury is traceable to the defendant, and that the injury can be redressed by a favorable ruling against the defendant. These are the constitutional requirements for standing under Article III. In addition to the constitutional requirements, courts have established prudential limitations that must also be met to establish standing. These prudential limitations include the following requirements: (1) the parties may not sue for a generalized grievance; (2) the plaintiff's complaint must be within the "zone of interests" protected by the statute at issue; and (3) the parties are generally prohibited from bringing a suit to protect the legal interests of a third party. While the constitutional requirements are unchangeable, Congress has the authority to limit the prudential requirements by granting an express cause of action within the statute at issue.

The Injury in Fact Requirement

The greatest barrier that people and organizations bringing suit on behalf of animals face in meeting the constitutional requirements of standing is the injury-in-fact requirement. Usually the injury is directly suffered by the animals and not by the people or organizations that are bringing suit on their behalf. In pleading such suits, the plaintiffs may not base their standing to sue on harm caused to the animal. Instead, they must allege a direct injury to themselves.

There are indeed many instances where people are able to bring suit to protect the interests of one who is not in a position to do so himself. For example, capable people may act as guardians and bring suit on behalf of children or the mentally handicapped. In those suits, the guardians have standing based on the injuries that happened directly to the ward because the ward has legally cognizable interests that he or she is entitled to have protected. . . .

In cases involving animals, the person or organization bringing suit is similarly trying to protect a being which cannot voice its own concerns in a court of law. In contrast to cases being brought by guardians of children or the mentally handicapped, because animals have no independent legal interests due to their classification as property, the plaintiff cannot simply plead that the animal is suffering an injury as a guardian can do for a ward. The plaintiff must instead plead an injury to himself that is independent from the injury to the animal.

Conditions at Edward Taub's Lab

For example, in *International Primate Protection League v. Institute for Behavioral Research, Inc.*, plaintiff Pacheco, a former employee of the defendant, together with animal rights organizations, brought suit under the Animal Welfare Act to become the guardians of monkeys that were being experimented on in a particularly cruel manner. The monkeys allegedly were given inadequate food and water and were kept in unsanitary conditions. One primatologist stated that he had "never seen a laboratory as poorly maintained [as that of the Institute for Behavioral Research]." Monkeys reportedly chewed their own fingers and further mutilated their limbs that had been experimented on. The defendant-institute's inhumane treatment of the monkeys was probably most strongly demonstrated by the fact that Dr. Edward Taub, the chief experimenter at the Institute, kept a hand that he had amputated from one of the monkeys as a paperweight on his desk. Despite these conditions, the United States Department of Agriculture ("USDA"), responsible for enforcing the Animal Welfare Act, found no violations of the Act. Pacheco provided his information to the police who ultimately seized the monkeys, and the monkeys were given temporarily to the care of an animal activist.

Despite the cruel treatment of the animals and the fact that the purpose of the Animal Welfare Act is, in part, "to insure that animals intended for use in research facilities . . . are provided humane care and treatment," the plaintiffs nonetheless had to plead standing based on an injury to themselves. They attempted to prove injury in fact on three separate bases. First, they claimed a financial interest as taxpayers in ensuring that the National Institutes of Health, which funded the experiments, respected the law. This claim was rejected essentially as a generalized taxpayer claim. Second, they argued that they had personal interests in the humane treatment of animals. This basis was held to be inadequate based upon the Supreme Court's holding in *Sierra Club v. Morton*, in which the Court denied standing based upon "a mere 'interest in a problem.'" Finally, the plaintiffs tried to counter directly the concerns of *Sierra Club* and argued that their personal relationships with the monkeys would be upset if the monkeys were returned to the Institute, thereby arguing a more direct, specific injury to themselves. The court replied that this case is distinguishable from *Sierra Club* because the plaintiffs in *Sierra Club* were litigating over an issue involving a national park and they could continue to use the park if the defendants complied with the law. The plaintiffs in *International Primate Protection*, however, would never be able to see the monkeys even if the defendants complied.

International Primate Protection highlights the treatment of animals as property in the context of standing in two distinct ways. First, in pleading standing, the plaintiffs had to establish injuries that occurred to *themselves*, when clearly the intention of their litigation was to prevent further injuries to the animals undergoing the abuse. Essentially, the plaintiffs had to contrive an injury that affected *people* so that the true injury—the abuse of the *animals*—could be stopped. Second, in denying standing because the plaintiffs would never see the monkeys again, the court was essentially creating a barrier against enforcement of the Animal Welfare Act and sanctioning abuse when animals are owned as private property. This is because private ownership precludes any further direct interaction between the plaintiffs and the privately owned animals and thus bars any possibility of showing a continuing harm. Under the court's logic, "because the monkeys were the private property of [the Institute for Behavioral Research], no private person or organization could claim standing to challenge the treatment of what the court essentially regarded as pieces of property." . . .

Owners Are Often Abusers

The Supreme Court has stated that the "[s]tanding doctrine ensures, among other things, that the resources of the federal courts are devoted to disputes in which the parties have a concrete stake." Moreover, it has held that "[t]he plaintiff must have a 'personal stake in the outcome' sufficient to 'assure that concrete adverseness which sharpens the presentation of issues upon which the court so largely depends for illumination of difficult . . . questions.'" The Supreme Court has therefore emphasized that the doctrine of standing requires conflict between the parties so that the parties will be zealously represented and the real issues of the case will come to light.

In the case of animals that are abused, however, those basic tenets of the standing doctrine are marginalized. Under a strict property interpretation, the owner of an animal experiences the most direct injury when the animal is abused, and thus the owner is the most logical plaintiff. In most suits involving mistreatment of animals, however, it is the *owner himself* who is the *abuser*. Therefore, the owner of the animal is the one who could most zealously argue for the termination of the abuse of the animal because he has borne the injury due to the abuse of his own property; however, the owner is *also* the party who would most often *inflict* the abuse upon the animal that is the very cause of the lawsuit.

In *International Primate Protection League v. Institute for Behavioral Research, Inc.*, the plaintiffs brought suit under the Animal Welfare Act for horrific abuses taking place against primates in a research facility. Under a strict property perspective, the Institute for Behavioral Research ("IBR") could have best advocated for the position that there had been violations of the Animal Welfare Act. If the monkeys are to be seen as purely personal property, then the abuse of the animals would have devalued the IBR's asset (the monkeys), and IBR, as the owner, would have been in the best position to advocate for the protection of the animals—its property—against mistreatment. It was precisely the IBR, however, that was inflicting the abuse. Thus, under a position that categorizes animals as pure property, the owner of the animal is often the best party to bring the suit *and* the best party to defend the suit. Such a result is inconsistent with the aforementioned tenets of the standing doctrine.

If, on the other hand, courts recognize that animals are indeed different than other types of property, the standing doctrine can be preserved in cases involving animals. By altering the perspective of these suits from one based purely on notions of property and toward one that recognizes that animals are indeed something more than ordinary personal property, this contradiction in the common law can be cured. If courts continue to ignore this crucial distinction and treat animals as if they are *not* qualitatively distinct from the typical piece of personal property, they are furthering a legal fiction and will continue to render decisions that do not comport with their own common law standing doctrine, which requires zealous representation of adverse interests. Once the courts recognize that animals—as distinct from other inanimate objects—do indeed have interests worthy of protection, the person who is best suited to protecting that interest is someone *other than the property owner* because it is normally the owner of the animal who is responsible for the abuse in the first place. Thus courts must retreat from their categorization of animals as solely property when evaluating issues of standing in order to abide by their own standing doctrine. . . .

Animals Differ from Other Property

It is evident that the legislature has . . . recognized that animals are worthy of protection by enacting statutes designed to protect animals, perhaps most obviously through the Animal Welfare Act. While the courts have not always been effective in upholding the spirit of animal welfare laws, it is clear that the laws are passed by the legislature to afford a special level of protection to animals that is not given to inanimate objects.

The courts should recognize that animals are qualitatively distinguishable from other types of personal property in deciding whether those who bring suit on behalf of mistreated animals have standing. If courts continue to disregard the obvious fact that animals are not only pieces of property but also that they have additional features that make them much more than property, they will continue to support a system of false pleadings, which does not address the real interests of the suits.

It is abundantly clear that animals are more than simply property. Yet in deciding whether those bringing suit on behalf of abused animals have standing, that fact is overwhelmed by the classification of the animals as property, and the animal's interests—which, at a minimum, include the right to be free from physical abuse—are not protected. Courts must recognize the interests of animals in order to stop furthering the "standing" fiction that exists with regard to animals and to comply with the courts' own standing doctrine. People or organizations should be able to present the injury to the animal directly in their pleadings as the injury in fact and should be permitted to act in their capacity as guardian or representative of the animal. Just as guardians of minor children are permitted to bring suit on behalf of those children without pleading a separate injury to themselves, courts should allow people and organizations to bring suit on behalf of animals without having to plead an injury separate from the abuse of the animals. To do so, courts would not have to overturn the common law, which recognizes animals as property. Instead courts would just have to recognize the obvious—animals are *more than* the average inanimate piece of personal property and they truly have cognizable interests worthy of protection.

Some Rare Cases

No discussion of animals and standing would be complete without mentioning that there have been rare cases in which animals have been held to have standing. While the overwhelming number of decisions has denied standing directly to animals, there have been rare instances in which animals have *themselves* brought suit, most typically under the Endangered Species Act. In those cases where animals successfully sued, their standing was not challenged by the defendants and the issue was not raised by the courts sua sponte [of their own accord]. In the cases where the standing of animals was actually considered by the court and the animals were granted standing, the holdings have been heavily criticized as a misinterpretation of the Endangered Species Act. Therefore, those cases in which animals or species of animals were granted standing, while noteworthy in a limited sense, do not create any real precedent upon which to base an argument that animals should have standing. This is largely because "animal species have remained named plaintiffs in . . . cases in which the defendants did not contest the issue," but "in the only reported case in which the naming of an animal as a party was challenged, the court found that the animal did not have standing to bring suit."

Whenever the case law on this issue has been assessed directly by the courts, they have found the cases granting standing to animals to be without any real impact on their decisions because in those cases, standing was simply unchallenged. No decision has been more significant in this respect than *Cetacean Community v. Bush*, in which the Ninth Circuit significantly limited its earlier holding in *Palila v. Hawaii Department of Land & Natural Resources*. In *Palila*, a species of bird was directly granted standing in its own right. In *Cetacean Community*, the Ninth Circuit stated that its earlier statements in *Palila* were "nonbinding dicta," noting that when it wrote its opinion, three other published opinions on the case had already been issued. Because the standing of the other parties was undisputed and the court was never asked to decide the standing of the species, the court explained that it had the jurisdiction to hear the case without considering whether the species of bird itself had standing. Thus, the court's statements in *Palila* regarding the standing of the species of bird were "little more than rhetorical flourishes. They were certainly not intended to be a statement of law, binding on future panels, that animals have standing to bring suit in their own name under the [Endangered Species Act]." . . .

Animals Are Worthy of Protection

It is widely accepted that animals are viewed as property under the law. It is equally apparent, however, that animals are much more than the average inanimate piece of personal property. The law of standing should reflect that animals are creatures with interests worthy of legal protection in their own right. Thus, while the courts may inevitably continue to recognize animals as property, animals are qualitatively different and the courts can and must take this into consideration when deciding the issue of standing. It is critical that courts allow people and organizations acting on behalf of an animal's best interest—as opposed to the property owner himself—to bring suit based on the injury to the animal. Limiting the party who can bring suit to the owner of the animal contradicts the standing doctrine because the property owner is typically the one inflicting the abuse. He will not zealously represent the interests of the animal because he would be arguing against his own abusive behaviors.

The common law has proven itself willing to progress with social and philosophical advancements and has embraced the idea that animals have independent interests that are worthy of protection. The idea that animals should be protected if and only if a human being is adversely affected is antiquated, inhumane, and out of step with reality. Thus, judges must continue to become more progressive when considering whether there is an injury in fact and consider that the animals themselves have interests entitled to legal protection.

> "A scientist who knew vital information about how to bring about recovery from a stroke became one of the most hated men in the United States, thanks in large part to a science establishment that chose to cater to an anti-human cause."

The Research Done on the Silver Spring Monkeys Led to an Important Discovery

Denyse O'Leary

Denyse O'Leary is a Canadian journalist and the coauthor of The Spiritual Brain: A Neuroscientist's Case for the Existence of the Soul. *In the following viewpoint she discusses the experience of Edward Taub, the scientist who did research on the Silver Spring monkeys. She describes him as a pioneer in the field now known as neuroplasticity. Before Taub's research, neuroscientists believed that the brain does not change during adult life. Most did not want to accept his ideas. Then, when he began experiments to investigate those ideas, he was arrested for cruelty to animals as a result of animal rights activists' desire to make his monkeys a rallying cry for their campaign. Scientists turned against him—in O'Leary's opinion, because they feared they might be the next victims—and he lost his reputation and his job. He spent many years and most of his money in an effort to*

Denyse O'Leary, "A Christmas Tale: Neuroscientist Discovers Hope for Stroke Victims—and Science Establishment's Hostility," *Mindful Hack* (blog), December 26, 2008. Reproduced by permission.

clear himself. Eventually, however, he was exonerated and was able to open a clinic, where he is applying what he learned through his experiments to the rehabilitation of stroke victims.

I've been reading Norman Doidge's *The Brain that Changes Itself*, and in Chapter 5, Midnight Resurrections, he tells the compelling story of Edward Taub, who bucked the establishment and won.

In the mid-twentieth century, a central dogma of neuroscience was that the brain does not change. This had a major impact in decision-making about treatment for strokes and other disorders that create brain damage. Treatment was deemed useless, and patients were typically warehoused in chronic care centres.

I remember this well because in 1966 I was a teenage volunteer in one such centre in Toronto—rows and rows of closely packed beds. Curiously, one patient (among many hundreds) had simply got better on her own and went home. It was considered a near miracle that gave much hope to the hard-pressed staff. I wonder, looking back, whether she had figured out something on her own—but not being an educated or prominent woman, she then took her secret with her to her grave. Here's why I wonder about that:

Early in his career, Taub started investigating neuroplasticity—a radical new idea that you change your brain according to what you think about. Some describe neuroplasticity as "use it or lose it" and others as "what you think about, so you become." Obviously, when we are discussing thinking, these two ideas are different ways of saying more or less the same thing. Of course, what makes the idea of neuroplasticity controversial is that it implies a subject who makes choices about what to think about—a non-materialist idea. But that is not the focus of this story.

Taub had, according to Doidge, started out in graduate school studying with behaviourists, who were interested neither in the mind nor in the brain, but only in measuring be-haviour, according to stimulus and response: You = Pavlov's dog in trousers.

Well, Taub realized that that idea wasn't really going any-where, so he made a risky choice—he took a job in an experi-mental neurology lab, to better understand the nervous sys-tem. This job included "deafferentation" experiments, using monkeys as subjects.

The basic idea is to sever the sensory nerves' connection with the brain, so the monkey no longer feels the limb. Typi-cally, the monkey stops moving the limb too, which doesn't completely make sense, as the motor nerves are not severed. Taub discovered, as a graduate student, that if he put a monkey's good arm in a sling, the monkey would start using the deafferented arm again. Essentially, the monkey had stopped using the deafferented arm as a form of learned be-haviour. It preferred the arm that continued to sense things (of course).

As Doidge puts it, Taub realized a couple of facts. One was that "behaviorism and neuroscience had been going down a blind alley for seventy years." There wasn't anything "hard-wired" about the monkeys' behaviour. They had simply made a choice; one that was reversible, given an incentive. Second, this finding could have dramatic implications for the treat-ment of brain damage in strokes. How much post-stroke pa-ralysis is learned paralysis? Learned, in the sense that—having failed to use faculties for many months—the patient no longer has the nervous system connections to make movement pos-sible or efficient. That was worth investigating.

Or so Taub thought. But he was mostly alone in that. Neuroscientists did not want to rethink their position on a fundamental issue, irrespective of what his findings clearly pointed to. "Most scientists in his field refused to believe his findings. He was attacked at scientific meetings and received no scientific recognition or awards." He was accused of "insolence" and had to get his PhD at New York State University rather than his original choice, Columbia.

There, Taub discovered by experiment that if the monkey was surgically deprived of feeling in both arms, it would use both arms. He had also learned, working with the monkeys, the importance of small rewards for just trying rather than a large reward for achievement. That insight could be put to use in developing exercises for humans as well.

The Persecution of Edward Taub

So, in May 1981, he found himself head of a Behavioral Biology Center in Silver Spring, Maryland, when Alex Pacheco, cofounder of People for the Ethical Treatment of Animals (PETA), took a job in his lab, professing an interest in medical research . . .

From Doidge:

> PETA was and is against *all* medical research involving animals, even research to cure cancers, heart disease, and AIDS
> . . . When Pacheco volunteered to work with Taub, his goal was to free the seventeen "Silver Spring monkeys" and make them a rallying cry for an animal rights campaign.

Pacheco got the police to seize the monkeys and got Taub arraigned for cruelty to animals. The science establishment, incredible as it may seem, chose to turn on Taub (fearing that they might be Pacheco's next victims, according to Doidge). Taub was arrested on 119 counts of cruelty to animals, losing his salary, his grants, and his lab privileges.

So a scientist who knew vital information about how to bring about recovery from a stroke became one of the most hated men in the United States, thanks in large part to a science establishment that chose to cater to an anti-human cause. Because that was the easy and safe thing to do. After all, it sounded good to Congressmen, pestered by animal activist constituents.

Taub spent the next six years of his life working sixteen hours a day, seven days a week, to clear himself, often functioning as his own lawyer. Before his trials began, he had $100,000 in life savings. By the end he had $4,000. Because he was blackballed, he couldn't get a job at a university. But gradually, trial by trial, appeal by appeal, charge, by charge, he refuted PETA.

Eventually, little thanks to the science establishment, Taub was able to open a clinic at the University of Alabama in [2001], and demonstrate that intensive rehabilitation (not half-hearted stuff mandated by a mediocre health insurance program) does reverse the supposedly permanent effects of many strokes. Early progress is slow because the affected arm has only half the original neurons to work with; effort restores the motor area of the brain to its normal size. Taub, having freed himself by his own efforts from the cowardice of the science establishment and the narrow fanaticism of anti-human cults, is currently studying optimum time periods for therapy.

CHAPTER 2

Animals Cannot Be Named as Plaintiffs in Lawsuits

Case Overview

Cetacean Community v. George W. Bush (2004)

Can animals be named as plaintiffs in lawsuits? Of course not, most people would say. Only human beings or organizations of human beings can be parties to legal action; however, some animal rights activists believe that this is wrong. They want to see the law changed to allow animals to sue. The animal rights movement favors giving *rights*, not merely good treatment, to animals.

In 2002 a suit was brought in the name of the "Cetacean Community"—that is, all whales and dolphins—against President George W. Bush and secretary of defense Donald Rumsfeld. It was filed by Lanny Sinkin, an environmentalist attorney who, with his wife, operates the Rainbow Friends Animal Sanctuary in Hilo, Hawaii. He wanted to call attention to the harm being done to cetaceans by the U.S. Navy's use of sonar. The filing stated:

> We, the Cetacean Community, come to this Honorable Court to offer what we consider a gift, not a complaint. The gift is the opportunity to expand the United States legal system to permit the Cetacean Community to bring suit on its own behalf. We consider this opportunity a gift because in granting standing to our community, you will be taking an evolutionary step for your own species. Extending Human recognition and respect to another species continues the Human process of moving beyond absorption with consumption of the Earth's resources to a broader view of Human responsibility as a steward and co-inhabitant of this planet with others.

The suit alleged that President Bush and Secretary Rumsfeld violated the National Environmental Policy Act (NEPA) by failing to prepare an environmental impact statement (EIS) for deployment of Low Frequency Active Sonar (LFAS) during threat and warfare conditions. It alleged that LFAS represents a significant threat to the cetacean community because this sonar "can disrupt critical behaviors, injure, and even kill." The suit asked the court to enter an injunction to prevent the use of sonar during threat and warfare conditions until the president and secretary of defense had prepared an EIS for use during such conditions in addition to the one prepared for sonar use during routine operations.

The judge dismissed the case, ruling that the cetaceans did not have standing to sue in their own name. Sinkin then took the case to the Ninth Circuit Court of Appeals, which considered the issue of standing very carefully. In a ruling that surprised most people and dismayed many, it ruled that animals cannot sue under any existing laws because they are not "persons"—but that under the Constitution there is no reason why Congress could not pass a law allowing them to sue if it wanted to. Thus, although the case was not permitted to go forward, activists were pleased by the statement that in principle, animals could be given some legal rights in the future.

It is not likely that this will happen, for if Congress tried to pass such a law there would be strong opposition. Many people believe that the Court misinterpreted the Constitution. "I think I lost because if the Ninth Circuit came out and said whales can sue [President] Bush, every talk show would trash this court," said Sinkin.

However, although lawsuits cannot be filed in the name of the cetaceans, the harm to them from sonar has been considered in many suits that humans have brought on their behalf.

> "If Congress and the President intended
> to take the extraordinary step of au-
> thorizing animals as well as people and
> legal entities to sue, they could, and
> should, have said so plainly."

The Court's Opinion: Animals Do Not Have Standing to Bring Suit

William A. Fletcher

William A. Fletcher has been a judge on the Ninth Circuit Court of Appeals since 1998. He is an outspoken member of the American Constitution Society, a nationwide association of liberal attorneys, judges, law students, and politicians. In the following opinion in Cetacean Community v. George W. Bush *he explains why the court ruled that cetaceans (marine mammals) cannot bring lawsuits in their own name. In a previous case, the court had commented that a bird, the Hawaiian palila, had legal status as a plaintiff in its own right, leading animal rights advocates to hope that this set a precedent. Fletcher asserts, however, that the statement about the Palila was not binding because it was merely a "rhetorical flourish" not necessary to the decision in that case. He states that there is nothing in the Constitution that would prevent Congress from giving animals the right to sue, but that Congress has not passed any laws that actually do so. Therefore, cetaceans do not have legal standing.*

William A. Fletcher, opinion, *Cetacean Community v. George W. Bush*, U.S. Court of Appeals for the Ninth Circuit, October 20, 2004.

W e are asked to decide whether the world's cetaceans [marine mammals] have standing to bring suit in their own name under the Endangered Species Act, the Marine Mammal Protection Act, the National Environmental Protection Act, and the Administrative Procedure Act. We hold that cetaceans do not have standing under these statutes.

The sole plaintiff in this case is the Cetacean Community ("Cetaceans"). The Cetacean Community is the name chosen by the Cetaceans' self-appointed attorney for all of the world's whales, porpoises, and dolphins. The Cetaceans challenge the United States Navy's use of Surveillance Towed Array Sensor System Low Frequency Active Sonar ("SURTASS LFAS") during wartime or heightened threat conditions. The Cetaceans allege that the Navy has violated, or will violate, the Endangered Species Act ("ESA"), the Marine Mammal Protection Act ("MMPA"), and the National Environmental Policy Act ("NEPA").

The Navy has developed SURTASS LFAS to assist in detecting quiet submarines at long range. This sonar has both active and passive components. The active component consists of low frequency underwater transmitters. These transmitters emit loud sonar pulses, or "pings," that can travel hundreds of miles through the water. The passive listening component consists of hydrophones that detect pings returning as echoes. Through their attorney, the Cetaceans contend that SURTASS LFAS harms them by causing tissue damage and other serious injuries, and by disrupting biologically important behaviors including feeding and mating.

The negative effects of underwater noise on marine life are well recognized. An analysis accompanying the current regulations for the Navy's use of SURTASS LFAS summarizes the harmful effects as follows:

> [A]ny human-made noise that is strong enough to be heard
> has the potential to reduce (mask) the ability of marine
> mammals to hear natural sounds at similar frequencies, in-

cluding calls from conspecifics, echolocation sounds of ond-
ontocetes, and environmental sounds such as surf noise. . . .
[V]ery strong sounds have the potential to cause temporary
or permanent reduction in hearing sensitivity. In addition,
intense acoustic or explosive events may cause trauma to tis-
sues associated with organs vital for hearing, sound production, respiration, and other functions. This trauma may include minor to severe hemorrhage.

The current regulations, governing routine peacetime
training and testing, have been challenged in a separate action. *Natural Res. Def. Council, Inc. v. Evans*, ("NRDC")
(issuing permanent injunction restricting the Navy's routine
peacetime use of LFA sonar "in areas that are particularly rich
in marine life").

The Cetaceans do not challenge the current regulations.
Instead, they seek to compel President [George W.] Bush and
Secretary of Defense [Donald] Rumsfeld to undertake regulatory review of use of SURTASS LFAS during threat and wartime conditions. The Navy has specifically excepted such use
of SURTASS LFAS from the current regulations. The Cetaceans seek an injunction ordering the President and the Secretary of Defense to consult with the National Marine Fisheries
Service under the ESA, to apply for a letter of authorization
under the MMPA, and to prepare an environmental impact
statement under NEPA. They also seek an injunction banning
use of SURTASS LFAS until the President and the Secretary of
Defense comply with what the Cetaceans contend these statutes command.

Defendants moved to dismiss the Cetaceans' suit under
Federal Rules of Civil Procedure 12(b)(1) for lack of subject
matter jurisdiction and 12(b)(6) for failure to state a claim
upon which relief can be granted. Without specifying which
of these rules was the basis for its decision, the district court
granted the motion to dismiss. The court held, *inter alia*

[among other things], that the Cetaceans lacked standing under the ESA, the MMPA, NEPA and the Administrative Procedure Act ("APA"). . . .

The Decision in *Palila IV*

The Cetaceans contend that an earlier decision of this court requires us to hold that they have standing under the ESA. We first address that decision. *Palila v. Hawaii Department of Land and Natural Resources*, ("*Palila IV*"), a suit to enforce the ESA, we wrote that an endangered member of the honeycreeper family, the Hawaiian Palila bird, "has legal status and wings its way into federal court as a plaintiff in its own right." We wrote, further, that the Palila had "earned the right to be capitalized since it is a party to these proceedings."

If these statements in *Palila IV* constitute a holding that an endangered species has standing to sue to enforce the ESA, they are binding on us in this proceeding. The government argues that these statements in *Palila IV* are nonbinding dicta. The district court agreed with the government's argument. However, at least two district courts, relying on our statements in *Palila IV*, have held that the ESA grants standing to animals. . . .

After due consideration, we agree with the district court that *Palila IV*'s statements are nonbinding dicta. A statement is dictum when it is "'made during the course of delivering a judicial opinion, but . . . is unnecessary to the decision in the case and [is] therefore not precedential.'" *Black's Law Dictionary*. The line is not always easy to draw, however, for "where a panel confronts an issue germane to the eventual resolution of the case, and resolves it after reasoned consideration in a published opinion, that ruling becomes the law of the circuit, regardless of whether doing so is necessary in some strict logical sense." *United States v. Johnson*.

When we decided *Palila IV*, the case had already been the subject of three published opinions, two by the district court and one by this court. Standing for most of the plaintiffs had always been clear, and standing for the Palila had never been a disputed issue. . . .

We have jurisdiction if at least one named plaintiff has standing to sue, even if another named plaintiff in the suit does not. Because the standing of most of the other parties was undisputed in *Palila I–IV*, no jurisdictional concerns obliged us to consider whether the Palila had standing. Moreover, we were never asked to decide whether the Palila had standing.

In context, our statements in *Palila IV* were little more than rhetorical flourishes. They were certainly not intended to be a statement of law, binding on future panels, that animals have standing to bring suit in their own name under the ESA. Because we did not hold in *Palila IV* that animals have standing to sue in their own names under the ESA, we address that question as a matter of first impression here.

Standing

Standing involves two distinct inquiries. First, an Article III [of the Constitution] federal court must ask whether a plaintiff has suffered sufficient injury to satisfy the "case or controversy" requirement of Article III. To satisfy Article III, a plaintiff "must show that (1) it has suffered an 'injury in fact' that is (a) concrete and particularized and (b) actual or imminent, not conjectural or hypothetical; (2) the injury is fairly traceable to the challenged action of the defendant; and (3) it is likely, as opposed to merely speculative, that the injury will be redressed by a favorable decision." *Friends of the Earth, Inc. v. Laidlaw Envtl. Sys.* If a plaintiff lacks Article III standing, Congress may not confer standing on that plaintiff by statute. A suit brought by a plaintiff without Article III standing is not a "case or controversy," and an Article III federal court therefore lacks subject matter jurisdiction over the suit. In that event, the suit should be dismissed under Rule 12(b)(1).

Second, if a plaintiff has suffered sufficient injury to satisfy Article III, a federal court must ask whether a statute has conferred "standing" on that plaintiff. Non-constitutional standing exists when "a particular plaintiff has been granted a right to sue by the specific statute under which he or she brings suit." *Sausalito* [*v. O'Neill*]. To ensure enforcement of statutorily created duties, Congress may confer standing as it sees fit on any plaintiff who satisfies Article III. Where it is arguable whether a plaintiff has suffered sufficient injury to satisfy Article III, the Supreme Court has sometimes insisted as a matter of "prudence" that Congress make its intention clear before it will construe a statute to confer standing on a particular plaintiff. If a plaintiff has suffered sufficient injury to satisfy the jurisdictional requirement of Article III but Congress has not granted statutory standing, that plaintiff cannot state a claim upon which relief can be granted. . . .

Article III Standing

Article III does not compel the conclusion that a statutorily authorized suit in the name of an animal is not a "case or controversy." As commentators have observed, nothing in the text of Article III explicitly limits the ability to bring a claim in federal court to humans.

Animals have many legal rights, protected under both federal and state laws. In some instances, criminal statutes punish those who violate statutory duties that protect animals. In other instances, humans whose interests are affected by the existence or welfare of animals are granted standing to bring civil suits to enforce statutory duties that protect these animals. The ESA and the MMPA are good examples of such statutes.

It is obvious that an animal cannot function as a plaintiff in the same manner as a juridically competent human being. But we see no reason why Article III prevents Congress from authorizing a suit in the name of an animal, any more than it prevents suits brought in the name of artificial persons such as corporations, partnerships or trusts, and even ships, or of juridically incompetent persons such as infants, juveniles, and mental incompetents.

If Article III does not prevent Congress from granting standing to an animal by statutorily authorizing a suit in its name, the question becomes whether Congress has passed a statute actually doing so. We therefore turn to whether Congress has granted standing to the Cetaceans under the ESA, the MMPA, NEPA, read either on their own, or through the gloss of Section 10(a) of the APA.

The APA

Section 10(a) of the APA provides:

A person suffering legal wrong because of agency action, or adversely affected or aggrieved by agency action within the meaning of a relevant statute, is entitled to judicial review thereof.

When a plaintiff seeks to challenge federal administrative action, Section 10(a) provides a mechanism to enforce the underlying substantive statute. Section 10(a) grants standing to any person "adversely affected or aggrieved by a relevant statute," making the relevant inquiry whether the plaintiff is hurt within the meaning of that underlying statute. . . .

The ESA

The ESA contains an explicit provision granting standing to enforce the duties created by the statute. The ESA's citizen-suit provision states that "any person" may "commence a civil suit on his own behalf . . . to enjoin any person, including the United States and any other governmental instrumentality or agency . . . who is alleged to be in violation of any provision of this chapter or regulation. . . ." The ESA contains an explicit definition of the "person" who is authorized to enforce the statute:

The term "person" means an individual, corporation, partnership, trust, association, or any other private entity; or any officer, employee, agent, department, or instrumentality of the Federal Government, or any State, municipality, or political subdivision of a State, or of any foreign government; any State, municipality, or political subdivision of a State; or any other entity subject to the jurisdiction of the United States.

The ESA also contains separate definitions of "species," "endangered species," "threatened species," and "fish and wildlife." . . .

It is obvious both from the scheme of the statute, as well as from the statute's explicit definitions of its terms, that animals are the protected rather than the protectors. The scheme of the ESA is that a "person," as defined in § 1532(13), may sue in federal district court to enforce the duties the statute prescribes. Those duties protect animals who are "endangered" or "threatened". The statute is set up to authorize "persons" to sue to protect animals whenever those animals are "endangered" or "threatened." Animals are not authorized to sue in their own names to protect themselves. There is no hint in the definition of "person" in § 1532(13) that the "person" authorized to bring suit to protect an endangered or threatened species can be an animal that is itself endangered or threatened.

We get the same answer if we read the ESA through Section 10(a) of the APA. The Supreme Court has specifically instructed us that standing under the ESA is broader than under the APA's "zone of interests" test. Moreover, like the ESA, Section 10(a) of the APA grants standing to a "person." "Person" is explicitly defined to include "an individual, partnership, corporation, association, or public or private organization other than an agency." Notably absent from that definition is "animal." . . .

The MMPA

Unlike the ESA, the MMPA contains no explicit provision granting standing to enforce its duties. The MMPA imposes a moratorium on "taking" a marine mammal without a permit, and prohibits "incidental, but not intentional" takes without a letter of authorization. The statute defines "[to] take" as "[to] harass, hunt, capture, or kill" any marine mammal, or to attempt to do any of these things. The MMPA explicitly grants standing to seek judicial review to any permit applicant, and to a "party" opposed to such a permit. But the statute says nothing about the standing of a would-be party, such as the Cetaceans, who seek to compel someone to apply for a letter of authorization, or for a permit.

Relying on Section 10(a) of the APA ... we have held that affected "persons" with conservationist, aesthetic, recreational, or economic interests in the protection of marine mammals have standing to seek to compel someone to apply for a permit under the MMPA. But, as discussed above, Section 10(a) of the APA does not define "person" to include animals. No court has ever held that an animal—even a marine mammal whose protection is at stake—has standing to sue in its own name to require that a party seek a permit or letter of authorization under the MMPA. Absent a clear direction from Congress in either the MMPA or the APA, we hold that animals do not have standing to enforce the permit requirement of the MMPA.

NEPA

NEPA requires that an environmental impact statement ("EIS") be prepared for "major Federal actions significantly affecting the quality of the human environment. . . ." As is true of the MMPA, no provision of NEPA explicitly grants any person or entity standing to enforce the statute, but judicial enforcement of NEPA rights is available through the APA. Interpreting NEPA broadly, we have recognized standing for individuals and groups of individuals who sue to require preparation of an EIS, when they contend that a challenged federal action will adversely affect the environment. However, we see nothing in either NEPA or the APA that would permit us to hold that animals who are part of the environment have standing to bring suit on their own behalf.

The Cetaceans argue that even if individual cetaceans do not have standing, their group has standing as an "association" under the APA. We disagree. A generic requirement for associational standing is that an association's "members would otherwise have standing to sue in their own right." *Laidlaw*. As discussed above, individual animals do not have standing to sue under the ESA, the MMPA, NEPA and the APA. Nor can the Cetaceans establish first-party organizational standing as an association under the APA. The complaint presents no evidence that the Cetaceans comprise a formal association, nor can we read into the term "association" in the APA a desire by Congress to confer standing on a non-human species as a group, any more than we can read into the term "person" Congressional intent to confer standing on individual animals.

We agree with the district court in *Citizens to End Animal Suffering & Exploitation, Inc.*, that "[i]f Congress and the President intended to take the extraordinary step of authorizing animals as well as people and legal entities to sue, they could, and should, have said so plainly." In the absence of any such statement in the ESA, the MMPA, or NEPA, or the APA, we conclude that the Cetaceans do not have statutory standing to sue.

"This is the crack in the door that the [animal rights activists] need in order to impose their wildly radical view of the world upon the rest of us."

The *Cetacean* Ruling Opens the Door to Other Suits by Animals

John F. Tamburo

John F. Tamburo is the editor in chief and publisher of Conservativity.com, a webzine dealing with political topics. In the following viewpoint he expresses his dismay at the Ninth Circuit Court of Appeals' opinion in Cetacean Community v. George W. Bush. *He objects not to the holding, which he says was correct, but to the court's statement that nothing in the Constitution would prevent Congress from authorizing a suit in the name of an animal. This, he feels, is a dangerous misinterpretation of the Constitution because it implies that the holding restricts animals from suing under a law only when the word "person" is used to define who may be a plaintiff. He fears that unless the Supreme Court reviews the case and closes this loophole, animal rights activists will use it to bring suits that most people would consider ridiculous and will thereby impose extremist minority views on society.*

The 9th Circuit Court of Appeals refused to order a lower court to allow a lawsuit by—get this—*whales and dolphins*—against our President [George W. Bush]. OK, that

John F. Tamburo, "Dodging a Legal Bullet? No, It's Still Flying!" Conservativity.com, October 22, 2004. Reproduced by permission.

sounds as if it is a reasonable and wise decision. I beg to differ. It is the correct *holding*, the correct *result*. The decision itself shows why the extreme left is so loony. In *Cetacean Community v. Bush* (October 20, 2004), the panel stated the following:

> "It is obvious that an animal cannot function as a plaintiff in the same manner as a juridically competent human being. But we see no reason why Article III [of the Constitution] prevents Congress from authorizing a suit in the name of an animal, any more than it prevents suits brought in the name of artificial persons such as corporations, partnerships or trusts, and even ships, or of juridically incompetent persons such as infants, juveniles, and mental incompetents."

Seems innocuous at first blush. Read it again. A document that establishes the rights of people has been interpreted in that Circuit as implicitly allowing *animals* the right to sue! The extremists and terrorists in the "Animal Rights" contingent [ARs] must be preparing a party, complete with Tofu, cloth shoes, lots of veggies and champagne! Unless the Supreme Court grants Certiorari [review] to this case, and definitely establishes a boundary, the bullet we apparently dodged is still flying and looking for a heart to pierce.

A Door to Extremist Legal Action

This ruling is narrow enough to let the "fur fly," so to say. For example, the holding basically restricts animals from suing for statutory violations where the word "person" is used to define who may be a plaintiff. Will we see the left start to use more generic words in legislation that gives the right to sue? For example "A person may sue under this statute if . . ." may become "One may sue under this statute if . . ."

Moreover, what about the Constitution? The Seventh Amendment states: "In Suits at common law, where the value in controversy shall exceed twenty dollars, the right of trial by jury shall be preserved, and no fact tried by a jury, shall be otherwise re-examined in any Court of the United States, than according to the rules of the common law." By the logic in *Cetacean*, animals now have the right to a jury trial in any common law matter over $20!

So you tell me: How long will it be before [actress and animal rights activist] Pamela Anderson sues KFC in the name of the chickens that the billboards claim are scalded alive and debeaked painfully? Wrongful death, intentional infliction of emotional distress, and other torts are generally held at the *common law*. Can the Taco Bell dog maintain a common law suit for misappropriation of its likeness? Will PETA [People for the Ethical Treatment of Animals] file a civil rights class action on behalf of the elephants at Ringling Brothers Barnum & Bailey Circus? Can Dobermans and Boxers file a class action for the docking of tails and/or ears?

This holding would be hilarious were it not so scary. This is the crack in the door that the AR's need in order to impose their wildly radical view of the world upon the rest of us. These wild activist courts are the enablers of the Tyranny of the Minority. This is the poster child case for the proposition that strict constructionist judges [judges who interpret the Constitution according to its original meaning] are so very important to reasonable law and order.

> "Animal activists may one day regret a judicial decision bestowing equality to apes or whales if public outrage provides the springboard for a constitutional amendment clearing up this controversy."

Congress Does Not Have Authority to Give Animals the Right to Sue

Matthew Armstrong

Matthew Armstrong, now an environmental law attorney in Washington, D.C., was a student at the University of California Hastings College of Law in San Francisco when he wrote the following legal comment. In it, he argues that the Ninth Circuit Court of Appeals' grounds for saying that Congress could give animals the right to sue are not valid. He states that the Constitution gives Congress the authority to pass only laws related to interstate commerce, and the interests protected by present animal legislation, such as the Endangered Species Act, are based on the value of animals to humans, the loss of which could have an impact on interstate commerce. Animals' own interests, on the other hand, involve only issues such as wrongful death, which are covered by state rather than federal laws. Even if Congress could enable animals to sue, he says, it is unlikely that there would be much federal legislation doing so, because common sense shows that animals are not equal to humans. After criticiz-

Matthew Armstrong, "Cetacean Community v. Bush: The False Hope of Animal Rights Lingers On," *West-Northwest*, vol. 12, Spring 2006, p. 185, 194–201, 204. Copyright © 2006 by University of California, Hastings College of the Law. Reproduced from the Hastings West-Northwest Journal of Environmental Law and Policy by permission.

ing the arguments of writers who believe that such equality exists, he points out that the frequently used analogy between the civil rights and animal rights movements is offensive to African Americans and that public outrage might lead to a call for a constitutional amendment to clarify the issue.

Cass Sunstein, the noted legal scholar from the University of Chicago, considers the question of animal standing to be "a simmering dispute with a simple answer." That answer, according to Sunstein, is that animals lack standing simply because Congress has failed to confer a cause of action on animals. This notion has received support from the U.S. Court of Appeals for the Ninth Circuit, which has recently affirmed that Article III of the Constitution of the United States does not prevent Congress from statutorily granting standing to an animal.

This comment explores the reasoning behind the Ninth Circuit's decision in *Cetacean Community v. Bush*, and attempts to expose the fundamental flaws in the argument supporting animal standing. . . .

Consider the following hypothetical: A ship wrecks across a sandbar, stranding a soldier and an ape on a small, deserted island with nothing but a canteen of water and a rifle. Help will not arrive for two weeks. What is the soldier's duty to the ape? If one holds that the interests of the ape and of the soldier deserve equal consideration—that the ape and the soldier have the *same basic right to life and liberty*—then the soldier cannot shoot the ape to provide himself with sustenance for the two weeks on the island. Both the ape and the soldier have an equal interest in continuing to live in the future. One possible answer is that the soldier may simply wait for the ape, driven by hunger, to attack him and then shoot the ape in self-defense. One could play out this scenario one hundred times and the ape, prompted by no more than a "primal" desire to survive, would attempt to kill the soldier every time. There could be no reciprocal restraint, born out of a respect for the other individual's rights, because the ape is unaware that he owes any duty to the soldier.

Legality of Standing for Animals

According to the Ninth Circuit, the only thing standing between the status quo—that humanity's interests are pre-eminent—and the macabre standoff described above is the predilection of Congress toward the former. In a passage as remarkable for its brevity as for its lack of supporting precedent, the Ninth Circuit blithely asserts that "Article III [of the Constitution] does not prevent Congress from granting standing to an animal by statutorily authorizing a suit in its name." That is to say, the Cetacean Community could sue the Navy if Congress amended the ESA to afford animals a private right of action.

The Ninth Circuit supports this holding with three lines of reasoning: (1) nothing in the text of Article III explicitly limits the right to bring a claim in federal court to humans; (2) there is a history of statutorily granting rights to animals; and (3) while animals obviously cannot function as plaintiffs in the same manner as a juridically competent human being, neither can a corporation, an infant or a mentally retarded adult.

Limits Under the Commerce Clause

Article III does not mention "humans" or "persons" as the necessary source of a "case or controversy" over which the federal courts have constitutional jurisdiction. Thus, an animal might be able to clear the injury-in-fact, causation and redressability hurdles that Article III erects. Apart from the obvious and significant retort that the Founders could not possibly have intended animals to be a party to the legal rights, structural safeguards and legal procedures guaranteed by the Constitution, it is tempting to posit the question, as [David Schmahmann and Lori Polacheck] have: "What kind of free-ranging commissions of inquiry would courts become if the [constitutional] requirements of human standing were removed and any advocate or group of advocates purporting to speak for any animal were entitled judicial access to press the animal's rights and to argue the animal's case?"

In response, proponents of animal standing are quick to note that [as Katherine Burke has written] "[p]laintiffs may have constitutional standing, but without a recognizable cause of action to support their requests for judicial relief, courts will dismiss their claims." Thus, the constitutional standing that animals might achieve for the purposes of an ESA animal-suit case would be necessarily limited by the narrow cause of action created by that provision.

Perhaps, but does Congress have the legislative authority to bestow a cause of action on animals? While the injury required by Article III may exist solely by virtue of "statutes creating legal rights, the invasion of which creates standing," [*Lujan v. Defenders of Wildlife*] Congress must have the power under the Constitution to enact such legislation. ESA's regulation of private (i.e., non-governmental) action has been justified by Congress' "commerce power." Considering recent Supreme Court limitations on Congress' powers under the Commerce Clause, it is unlikely that Congress could justify an animal-suit statute.

Congress may traditionally pass laws regarding (1) "the use of the channels of interstate commerce"; (2) "the instrumentalities of interstate commerce, or persons or things in interstate commerce, even though the threat may come only from intrastate activities"; and (3) "those activities having a substantial relation to interstate commerce." The human injuries that Congress has recognized under the current version of the ESA are moored in the "esthetic, ecological, educational, historical, recreational, and scientific value [of endangered animals] to the Nation and its people." Courts have repeatedly recognized the effect of the loss of these values on interstate commerce, and so it is doubtful that the Court will invalidate the current ESA in its tightening of the Commerce Clause. But these justifications are invariably utilitarian, and the interests protected are not shared by animals. An animal has no esthetic, ecological, educational, historical, recreational or scientific interest in itself. It merely has a stake in its continued existence, and so an amendment to the ESA empowering animals to sue would create merely a tort claim for battery or wrongful death. Traditionally, the contours of criminal and civil actions based on purely intrastate violence are defined by the States.

Statutory vs. Guaranteed Rights

The second prong of the Ninth Circuit's reasoning relies on the fact that "[a]nimals have many legal rights, protected under both federal and state law." To support this assertion, the Ninth Circuit marshals the African Elephant Conservation Act, the Animal Welfare Act, the Horse Protection Act and the Wild Free-Roaming Horses and Burros Act. Surprisingly, the word "right" is not once used in conjunction with the term "animal" in any of these statutes. All the statutes regulate the capture, care, sale and purchase of various animals, and all frame the purposes of the statute in terms of the benefits Americans gain by the continued existence and humane treatment of these animals.

The Animal Welfare Act (AWA) is the broadest of these statutes. It governs the transportation, sale and handling of research animals, commercial livestock and domesticated pets. The stated purpose of the AWA is to "insure that animals intended for use in research facilities or for exhibition purposes or for use as pets are provided humane treatment and care." The AWA imposes criminal liability on those who violate the statutorily-imposed duties to the animals covered by the Act. The Ninth Circuit noted that other animal protection statutes, such as the ESA and MMPA, afford civil standing to humans to enforce the statutory duties imposed by those statutes.

But the Ninth Circuit uses circular reasoning: animals have rights because congressional statutes impose duties on people to treat animals a certain way; Congress can impose animal-enforced duties *because animals have rights.* The court reasons that the very existence of statutory protections such as those contained in the AWA is proof that Congress can recognize animal-injury as a sufficient predicate to create animal-standing. This argument should be revisited in light of the Commerce Clause problems discussed above. It is unclear that Congress can use animal-injury as an adequate justification for national legislation, at least insofar as that injury affects the animal rather than the researcher, cattleman or owner.

The Logistics of Animal Standing

The final barrier to Article III standing is a practical one. Animals cannot walk into a courthouse and file a claim on their own. The Ninth Circuit brushed aside this problem, writing that "we see no reason why Article III prevents Congress from authorizing a suit in the name of an animal, any more than it prevents suits brought in the name of artificial persons such as corporations, partnerships or trusts, and even ships, or of juridically incompetent persons such as infants, juveniles, and mental incompetents."

Use of this analogy as an argument for disregarding the practical inability of animals to articulate colorable claims is not new; it has been applied to rocks and trees as well. [Legal scholar] Christopher Stone recognized the temptation to distinguish between the corporate form—an entity created by humans to serve humans (much like our government and Constitutional Convention)—and environmental objects that lack any such justification for employing legal fictions to entertain suits. But, says Stone, "the more we learn about the sociology of the firm—and the realpolitik of our society—the more we discover the ultimate reality of these institutions, and the increasingly legal fictiveness of the individual human being." Presumably, Stone means that the corporation diffuses any individual human member's feeling of moral responsibility for its actions and, so divorced from the collective guiding conscience of its members, the corporation takes on a ruthless personality of its own.

This argument is not particularly convincing, especially as it is employed as support for the legal standing of animals. Stone's conclusions regarding the rudder of the corporate form are based on nothing more than conjecture and anecdote. Additionally, Stone seems to say that once our society perverts the legal system by allowing claims by entities beholden to no individual human interest, there can be no further harm in allowing others.

The point of this exercise is not to answer these questions, but simply to highlight the glaring absence of discussion or analysis in the Ninth Circuit's opinion. Because the Article III question is a prerequisite to deciding the case under the ESA, the unexamined statements by the Ninth Circuit will have to be interpreted as binding by the lower courts. It will not be as easy for the Ninth Circuit to sidestep these statements as it did its "rhetorical flourishes" of *Palila IV*.

Even so, there will not likely be a torrent of new federal legislation enabling animals to sue. The next section of this comment examines some of the philosophical debate raging on this issue. Given the controversy surrounding the grant of "animal rights" (not to mention the religious implications), it seems doubtful that Congress will delve into this contentious area. This comment argues that such caution is appropriate.

Philosophical Arguments

Even if Congress *could* bestow affirmative rights upon animals, common sense militates against it. Legal authority is understandably shallow in this area, but there are competing academic theories. One, espoused by Professor Sunstein, is that the capacity to suffer should provide a sufficient basis for legal rights for animals. Sunstein argues that "no one seriously urges that animals should lack legally enforceable claims against egregious cruelty, and animals have long had a wide range of rights against cruelty and mistreatment under [the law]." This aspect of Sunstein's argument is one which the Ninth Circuit appears to have adopted.

Another legal theory is vigorously pursued by Steven Wise in his controversial work, *Rattling the Cage: Toward Legal Rights for Animals*. Wise argues that chimpanzees and bonobos have sufficient mental ability to be deemed "legal persons" for the purposes of securing bodily integrity and bodily liberty. Wise's arguments have been lauded in many legal and political circles, and the book has spawned like-minded works.

The hypothetical exposes a fundamental philosophical flaw of extending abstract "rights" to animals. Laws, by which we preserve these rights, are artificial restraints on the natural impulses of human beings. Reciprocal restraint allows the formation of communities of humans that pursue selfish ends through, if not unselfish, at least tempered means. Not one of the articles cited [below] mentions any instance of an animal—even one that closely resembles humans, like an ape or chimpanzee—exercising restraint to the point of forfeiting existence to comply with an abstract agreement. No one has produced an example of an animal even *recognizing* an abstract agreement. At the very least, then, even if humans extend animals individual rights such as those we enjoy—to life, freedom, property—a human will always be capable of tricking an animal into forfeiting those rights by breaching the contract the animal is not even aware exists.

The response to the ape/soldier hypothetical above is that humans do not consider infants or the mentally-retarded to have sacrificed individual rights, even though an individual infant or mentally-deficient adult may be totally unable to exercise restraint. . . . Our society affords mentally-retarded adults, quite incapable of living on their own, the same basic rights of life and liberty enjoyed by its more fortunate and more rational members. Indeed, our society affords autonomy not only to those with low levels of actual autonomy, but to those without any actual autonomy at all. Wise argues that the legal fiction of the "autonomous" invalid demonstrates that "no bright line divides full autonomy from realistic autonomy or realistic autonomy from the legal fiction that 'all humans are autonomous.'"

The distinction between the infant and the animal should be easy to see: the infant will presumably go on to develop the cognitive ability to exercise restraint as he or she matures into an adult. Why would adult humans not afford infants the same fundamental rights they enjoy themselves? With the passage of years that infant will become an adult, replenish the adult population and contribute (perhaps) to the propagation of the species. The animal afforded the same rights will contribute none of these things. But, argues Wise, we do not qualify the equality of infants. Rather, we grant them full enjoyment of basic legal rights because of their potential to contribute to the success of the species.

The potentiality argument does not convince Wise:

"[i]f we accept the argument for potential autonomy, then both bonobo and child are entitled to dignity-rights. If we reject it, then neither is *entitled* to dignity rights. Whether one or both of them gets them will turn on the willingness of judges to use a legal fiction that one or both is autonomous until they actually become so."

An Offensive Comparison

To Wise, chimpanzees and infants are alike. "[A]t bottom," equality demands that "likes be treated alike." The fact that animals and infants are not treated alike is the result of species-centric thinking in which "for no good and sufficient reason, equality is violated." And, according to Wise:

> [E]quality destroyed anywhere, even for chimpanzees, threatens the destruction of equality everywhere. That is why, near the onset of the American Civil War, Abraham Lincoln told Congress that "[i]n giving freedom to the slave, we assure freedom to the free." To deny freedom to the slave, the confederacy had to shackle its white citizens. Had Pickett's Charge split the Union lines at Gettysburg, the American South might today be dotted with biomedical research laboratories using not just slaves, instead of nonhuman primates, but anyone that the government . . . thought most useful.

One can hardly imagine a comparison more offensive to African-American descendants of slaves than the analogy, frequently deployed today, between the civil rights movement and the animal rights movements. Stephen Wise has argued that society's current "oppression" of chimpanzees and bonobos is analogous to both slavery and the Holocaust, situations in which utility subordinated morality. This argument rests largely on the unprovable assumption that the moral difference between humans and chimpanzees is the product of species-centric bias on the part of humans. If the whole concept of "morality" is nothing more than a human construct, why should it not be species-centric? . . .

As has happened in the debate over same-sex marriage, animal activists may one day regret a judicial decision bestowing equality to apes or whales if public outrage provides the springboard for a constitutional amendment clearing up this controversy. Since the motivation of most animal rights activists seems to be the practical protection of animals rather than ideological "rightness," preserving the goodwill of the public may be more important than granting standing to the Cetacean Community.

> "The very creatures the Endangered Spe-
> cies Act was created to protect were de-
> nied protection because the Navy per-
> formed its sonar deployment in such a
> manner as to be as safe to humans as
> possible."

Cetacean Exemplifies the Difficulty of Suing for Harm to Nature

W. Earl Webster

At the time this article was written, W. Earl Webster was a student at the University of Utah College of Law. In the following viewpoint he explains that the case Friends of the Earth, Inc. v. Laidlaw Environmental Services *made it easier for citizens to bring environmental lawsuits by liberalizing the requirement for legal standing to sue. At the same time, however, it reduced the effectiveness of suing because it explicitly stated that only harm to the actual plaintiffs entitles them to file suit; harm to the environment is irrelevant. In Webster's opinion this is a bad thing because it places the focus on damage done to individuals rather than on that done to the common asset of nature. He uses* Cetacean Community v. Bush *as an example of the problem. In* Cetacean Community *marine mammals were denied standing to sue under the Endangered Species Act (ESA) in order to prevent sonar tests harmful to them, in part because of the ruling in* Laidlaw *since no humans could have been harmed by these tests. But many cetaceans were killed or maimed, he argues, in spite of the fact that the ESA was intended to protect them.*

W. Earl Webster, "How Can Mother Nature Get to Court?" *Journal of Land, Resources and Environmental Law,* vol. 27, 2007, pp. 453, 459–62. Reproduced by permission.

Unfortunately, the ideal of environmental caretaking envisioned in 1972 by an American literary icon never came to fruition. The venerable Dr. Seuss envisioned the environment protected by a Lorax—a being who would "speak for the trees, for the trees have no tongues." Dr. Seuss' Lorax is ignored until all the Truffula trees are harvested and the ecology is unbalanced and collapses. Today, those who would act as Lorax for our environment are not so much ignored as affirmatively muzzled by a Supreme Court that has crafted modern standing doctrine so as to exclude Nature from the judicial process. . . .

Finally, in 2000 the Court ceased its relentless efforts to constrict environmental standing and began to moderate the standing doctrine. In *Friends of the Earth, Inc. v. Laidlaw Environmental Services, Inc.* the Court again addressed the issue of standing once the defendant had become compliant during the course of litigation—this time in the context of the Clean Water Act. After an extensive review of the development of environmental standing law, the Court concluded Friends of the Earth did have standing because its members had demonstrated concrete, discrete harms experienced as a result of Laidlaw's actions.

The Court reiterated its three-part standing test from [*Lujan v.*] *Defenders of Wildlife*, but gave a much liberalized interpretation of how to apply the test. The Court loosened the injury in fact requirement so that the plaintiff need only show the defendant violated a law and the plaintiff was harmed thereby. Further, the Court limited the effects of *Steel Co.* [v. Citizens for a Better Environment] by holding that the deterrent effect inherent in civil penalties can be sufficient, standing alone, to meet the redressability requirement of the *Defenders of Wildlife* test.

Nature Only Partially Protected

By liberalizing the injury and redressability requirements of *Defenders of Wildlife, Laidlaw* definitely benefited environmental litigants. However, not only did *Laidlaw* not solve the problem of ensuring Mother Nature standing, it actually exacerbated the issue. Within its analysis the Court included the statement "[t]he relevant showing for purposes of Article III standing, however, *is not injury to the environment* but injury to the plaintiff." This sentence ensures that suits by humans who have been harmed by damage to the environment brought in their capacity as citizens of the United States have an easier row to hoe with respect to standing. Conversely, that same sentence guarantees that suits filed by humans on behalf of Nature, having been harmed by the actions of citizens of the United States, are essentially dead on arrival unless the harm extends to actual citizens.

Professor [David] Cassuto has indicted this sentence from *Laidlaw* as both illogical and internally inconsistent. His criticism begins with this observation:

> Both alone and in the context of the full opinion, this sentence exposes fundamental incoherencies within standing doctrine, especially with respect to standing's relationship with environmental law ... Declaiming that injury to the plaintiff rather than harm to environment comprises the requisite for standing enables the Court to ground its basis for standing in an opposition that makes no sense, even though it is firmly grounded in precedent. In other words, the sentence (and, consequently, the rest of the opinion) is simultaneously legally strong and rhetorically incoherent.

Cassuto buttresses this statement by extensively developing several reasons the Court's focus on harm to the plaintiff rather than the environment is a mistake. Only brief summaries of those arguments can be presented here.

First, Cassuto argues that the entirety of society is a single system comprised of myriad components. Since harm to any one of those components harms the entire system, which component is harmed should be irrelevant when determining legal standing. As a system-critical component, the environment should be considered worthy of standing just like any other component.

Second, the plaintiff-harm focus actually complicates litigations by diverting attention away from the common asset environmental laws seek to protect and focusing that attention on harm experienced by a few individuals. Thus, the very objectives of environmental litigation become skewed.

Third, this skewing of objective, coupled with a traditional private-property decision paradigm, actually results in partial evisceration of the effectiveness of citizen suits as a means of protecting the environment. Finally, focusing on the plaintiff's harm renders any harm analysis overly subjective by focusing on the wrong entity (Nature is the entity that is actually being harmed), thus mooting the entire analysis.

The *Cetacean Community* Case

An example case, *The Cetacean Community v. Bush*, demonstrates the problems created by *Laidlaw's* anthropocentric holding. In 2003, counsel for the Cetacean Community—an association of all wild whales, dolphins, and porpoises in the world's oceans—filed suit under the Endangered Species Act against President George W. Bush and Secretary of Defense Donald Rumsfeld to enjoin the United States Navy's use of certain types of sonar that had been shown to cause hearing impairment and death in cetacean species. The suit was brought solely on behalf of the cetaceans because the Navy had designed the deployment so as to drive the threat of harm to humans to its absolute minimum thus leaving the sea's cetacean population as the only creatures facing a meaningful risk of injury.

Addressing the issue of standing, the court found that nothing in the text of Article III [of the Constitution] explicitly limits standing to human plaintiffs. The court stated, "we see no reason why Article III prevents Congress from authorizing a suit in the name of an animal, any more than it prevents suits brought in the name of artificial persons such as corporations . . . or of juridically incompetent persons . . ." The court then proceeded to search for a statutory right of standing under any of the statutes cited by the plaintiffs. The court first considered the Endangered Species Act and concluded the ESA's citizen suit provisions cannot grant standing to nonhuman plaintiffs because they are not humans. The court also concluded the Marine Mammal Protection Act right of action that would arise through the Administrative Procedure Act (APA) cannot grant nonhuman plaintiffs standing because they are not humans. The court found the same for the National Environmental Policy Act. Finally, the court denied standing as an association under APA because *Laidlaw* requires the members of the association must have standing in their own right and nonhumans simply cannot have standing as individuals.

The detrimental paradox inherent in *Laidlaw*'s standing for humans but not for Nature can be seen in how harmful the sonar tests the Cetacean Community sought to enjoin proved to be. Truly, no humans were, nor could have been, harmed by the sonar tests. Conversely, substantial numbers of cetaceans were killed or maimed. Thus, the very creatures the Endangered Species Act was created to protect were denied protection because the Navy performed its sonar deployment in such a manner as to be as safe to humans as possible.

In the end, *The Cetacean Community* shows *Laidlaw* may have improved citizens' opportunities to obtain standing to enforce environmental legislation but it did nothing to assist Nature. In fact, Nature remains barred from the courts because the right to use the courts remains reserved solely to humans.

> *"Through the plaintiffs' capacity for em-*
> *pathy with the particular animals, vio-*
> *lations of animal rights become viola-*
> *tions of human interests, which can*
> *then be brought before the court."*

Human Plaintiffs Can Act as Proxies for Animals in Lawsuits

Harvard Law Review

In the following excerpt from an editorial in the Harvard Law Review, *the authors point out that in some recent court cases animals have been viewed as individuals, rather than just as species as they were in the past. To bring a lawsuit, a person or persons must have suffered, or be about to suffer, some kind of harm. In* Cetacean Community v. Bush *animals were denied the right to sue because although there was a prospect of their being harmed, they were not persons. There had been suits in which human plaintiffs were allowed to sue under the Endangered Species Act on account of potential interference with their "aesthetic interest" in observing animals. This had been interpreted as applying to endangered species, since if a species was harmed there would be fewer animals of that species left to observe. However, in several recent cases the plaintiffs have argued that they had an aesthetic interest in observing particular animals, such as those in a zoo where they were being mistreated. This has increased the protection of animals by the courts. In a*

Harvard Law Review, "Developments in the Law: Access to Courts," vol. 122, February 2009, pp. 1204–12. Copyright © 2009 by the Harvard Law Review Association. Republished with permission of Harvard Law Review, conveyed through Copyright Clearance Center, Inc.

sense, say the authors, humans have begun to act as proxies for animals that cannot sue in their own name.

Over the last forty years, federal law has conferred a wide range of rights on animals. This [viewpoint] explores one way in which private suits to enforce these rights gain access to federal courts: by alleging that the unlawful treatment of animals is causing "aesthetic injury" to a human plaintiff. This type of suit has long been used to enforce regulatory and statutory protections of ecosystems and species. But it is only in the last decade that courts have recognized this type of injury in suits aimed at protecting *individual* animals. If only individuals, and not groups, can have rights—as many rights theorists argue—this development may be significant, marking the beginning of a new form of judicial access for animals: via human proxy. However, there is a tension here, as the doctrinal development nominally pertains to persons alone. It is only through their transformation into harms to persons that violations of animal rights are remedied by the courts. Although classical animal rights theorists may see this as a crude legal device that fails to truly extend the protection of U.S. courts to animals, it is possible that such protection cannot, as these theorists suggest, be brought about by a change in the legal status of animals alone. What might also be necessary is a change in our human sensibilities. And this type of change might underlie the expansion of the "aesthetic injury" doctrine that can be seen in the cases discussed.

Animals in Court

In 1386, a female pig was put on trial in France for causing the death of a child by tearing his face and arms. Trials such as this were not uncommon in medieval Europe. The same procedural rules applied to human and animal defendants, and the defense counsel for animals often "raised complex legal arguments" on their behalf. In this case, the sow was found guilty, and true to *lex talionis*—the law of "eye-for-an-eye"—

the tribunal ordered that she be maimed in the head and upper limbs; after this, she was hanged in the public square.

Today, animals hold a very different place in our law: as the subjects of extensive federal protection and the beneficiaries of private trusts, they are no longer defendants, but rather, aspiring plaintiffs in U.S. courts. In *Palila v. Hawaii Department of Land & Natural Resources*, for example, an endangered bird species brought suit, along with environmental organizations, to enforce the Endangered Species Act. On appeal, the Ninth Circuit stated: "As an endangered species under the Endangered Species Act . . . , the bird . . . has legal status and wings its way into federal court as a plaintiff in its own right." Turtles, bears, squirrels, and various other bird species have likewise had their day in court. However, in these cases, human plaintiffs were also involved.

When courts have confronted cases in which animals were the sole plaintiffs, such as in *Cetacean Community v. Bush*, they have often held that animals were not authorized to bring suit in their own right. In *Cetacean Community*, the problem for the animal plaintiffs was that the statutes cited for causes of action authorize only "persons" to bring enforcement suits, and the court determined that animals do not fall into these statutes' definitions of "person."

This conclusion was not tautological, for one need not be a human to be a legal person: corporations and cities, for example, can be legal persons. But so far, the only animals that are "persons" are humans. Thus, although federal law recognizes "a wide range of animal rights," these rights are unlike the common law rights of humans in that animals cannot sue to enforce them. Enforcement is left primarily to governmental action, which may be supplemented by private claims when these are authorized by "citizen suit" provisions.

In addition to having a cause of action, a plaintiff must meet the requirements of constitutional and prudential standing. Under the Supreme Court's interpretation of Article III [of the Constitution], a plaintiff must demonstrate that he has "suffered an 'injury in fact' that is (a) concrete and particularized and (b) actual or imminent, not conjectural or hypothetical"; that the injury is "fairly traceable to the challenged action of the defendant"; and that it is "likely, as opposed to merely speculative, that the injury will be redressed by a favorable decision." The courts have also created "prudential" requirements, which Congress can eliminate when drafting a statute. The most important of these requires allegation of more than "a generally available grievance" shared by all or most citizens, and that this injury "falls within the 'zone of interests' sought to be protected by the statutory provision whose violation forms the legal basis for [the] complaint." [*Lujan v. National Wildlife Federation*]

The Law of Aesthetic Injury

In the past decade, the law of standing as it relates to claims about animal rights has undergone significant development through a series of appellate court cases. In *Animal Legal Defense Fund v. Glickman* and *Animal Legal Defense Fund v. Veneman*, the plaintiffs sued the U.S. Department of Agriculture on the grounds that its regulation of the treatment of particular primates in zoos violated the agency's statutory mandate under the Animal Welfare Act (AWA). And in *American Society for the Prevention of Cruelty to Animals v. Ringling Brothers and Barnum & Bailey Circus*, the plaintiffs sued a circus owner under the citizen suit provision of the Endangered Species Act (ESA), alleging that the circus mistreated particular elephants in violation of the statute. On the issue of standing, the plaintiffs in all three cases alleged particularized and concrete injury by virtue of the fact that they had developed personal attachments to the specific animals at issue. Thus, a central question in all of these cases was whether the plaintiffs could have a legally cognizable interest in the treatment of an individual animal.

In the core cases establishing the scope of aesthetic inter-ests—cases building on the Supreme Court's 1972 holding in *Sierra Club v. Morton*—species and ecosystems, not particular animals, were at issue. As a result, the legally cognizable aes-thetic interest in observing animals established by these cases was one of observing species: plaintiffs gained access to the court by virtue of the injuries they incurred as the result of defendants' actions that threatened to significantly diminish the species of animal. It was by characterizing their injury as "an increased probability of one kind or another," such as an increased chance that there would be fewer animals available for viewing, that the plaintiffs in these suits satisfied the stand-ing requirement. And in the view of some judges, diminution of the species was the "touchstone" of the law.

However, the courts in three recent cases reasoned that there could be no relevant distinction between harm to a spe-cies and harm to a particular animal. In the *Glickman* court's discussion of the standing of one plaintiff, it explained: "The key requirement ... is that the plaintiff have suffered his in-jury in a personal and individual way—for instance, by seeing with his own eyes the particular animals whose condition caused him aesthetic injury." Thus, the *Glickman* court held that the inhumane treatment of particular primates at the zoo could be the predicate of a legally cognizable aesthetic injury. And in *Veneman*, the court expressly articulated this point: "For purposes of injury-in-fact, a distinction between harm to individual animals, on the one hand, and harm to an animal species through diminution or extinction, on the other, is il-logical. The injury at issue is not the animals' but the human observer's."

While *Veneman* is primarily significant for its support of the *Glickman* holding, the *Ringling Brothers* court made a fur-ther impact on federal standing jurisprudence in the context of what might be considered animal rights cases. Unlike the plaintiff at issue in *Glickman*, the plaintiff in *Ringling Brothers* did not have concrete plans to continue seeing the elephants whose treatment caused his injury. He merely *wanted* to see them, and this fact is significant. When seeking injunctive relief, "harm in the past . . . is not enough to establish a present controversy, or in terms of standing, an injury in fact." The D.C. Circuit concluded, however, that this difference in imminence was not an insurmountable obstacle. The court drew on *Friends of the Earth v. Laidlaw Environmental Services*, a Supreme Court case holding that the plaintiffs suffered injury in fact when they desired to use and enjoy one of their favorite rivers for recreation but could not because it was polluted. The court concluded that "an injury in fact can be found when a defendant adversely affects a plaintiff's enjoyment of flora or fauna, which the plaintiff *wishes* to enjoy again upon the cessation of the defendant's actions." . . .

Animal Rights and Human Proxies

The fact that these cases involved individual animals, rather than species, is important, for it means that courts' doors are now open to citizen suits that might lead to the enforcement of animal rights. Although the aesthetic injury cases of the 1970s–1990s created and enforced new duties towards species and ecosystems—by either requiring the promulgation of new regulations or the enforcement of existing ones—these duties were not necessarily the correlatives of animal rights. The reason for this potential divergence is that a species, unlike an individual, is not an entity with coherent interests. For example, if an animal species will benefit from the selective killing of its members that are carrying a deleterious gene, the species and some of its members will have conflicting interests. In this case, as a practical matter, a duty to protect the species will not confer rights upon all of its members. Moreover, as a conceptual matter, the idea of "species rights" is—according to many rights theorists—nonsensical, the problem being that "[s]pecies and ecosystems are the names for global entities, to which the theory of rights is inapplicable." On this account, judicial enforcements of statutory duties to animals in the core aesthetic injury cases did not enforce animal rights. Seen in this context, *Glickman* and the cases following it are significant in that they open U.S. courts' doors to citizen suits in which animal rights are adjudicated. Whether this development should be seen as an advance in animals' access to the courts, however, is arguable. There are two very different ways to conceptualize this development.

On one account, these cases speak only to human interests and their enforcement by the courts. As Professor Cass Sunstein notes, having a legal interest in a dispute can be thought of as having a property interest at stake. Thus, one might suggest the legal effect of these cases is comparable to that of creating a new property right in animals that belongs not to the owner, but to the community—to those who view the animal (in the case of *Glickman*) and even to those who want to view the animal (in the case of *Ringling Brothers*). From this perspective, the development of the law in these cases is a further commodification of animals as legal things, not a shift to a recognition of them as rights-bearers. . . .

When seen functionally—with an eye to what is at stake and can be achieved—these cases impact not only the access of humans to courts, but also that of animals: through these developments in standing law, judges come to adjudicate a new class of claims about the statutory rights of privately owned animals and the adequacy of the regulations protecting them.

There is, moreover, a sense in which the plaintiffs in these cases can be seen as proxies for the animals that they brought suit to protect. In all three cases, the court's recognition of injury in fact was predicated on the specificity not only of the harm to the plaintiffs, but also of that to the animals. . . .

Although these courts' focus on the particularity of the animals does not make sense as a matter of law—for it is injury to the plaintiff, not the animal, that must be "concrete and particularized"—it points to an important feature of these suits. What seems to be going on in these cases, which did not occur in the earlier aesthetic injury cases regarding species protection, is that the plaintiffs are acting as proxies by which harms suffered by individual animals are translated into human harms. Through the plaintiffs' capacity for empathy with the particular animals, violations of animal rights become violations of human interests, which can then be brought before the court.

CHAPTER 3

Routine Farming Practices Are Subject to Anticruelty Regulations

Case Overview

New Jersey Society for the Prevention of Cruelty to Animals et al. v. New Jersey Department of Agriculture (2008)

In recent years the public has become increasingly concerned about the welfare of farm animals. This is due in part to agitation by animal rights activists, who do not believe animals or their products should be eaten. A much larger number of people are dismayed by the way animals used for food are raised and slaughtered. The picture most have of farming has been based on family farms, where relatively few animals were kept in pens or pastures and could move around freely, but these are largely a thing of the past. In the United States and Europe today, food is produced mainly through "factory farming," which is the practice of confining large numbers of cows, pigs, chickens, or turkeys in small indoor spaces. This is necessary, it is argued, in order to feed growing populations and to keep costs down; however, it means that the animals cannot behave as they would naturally. In some cases, they are kept in individual cages or pens so small that they cannot even turn around.

Factory farming is controversial. Many agricultural experts believe that the animals are better off being in environmentally controlled housing, protected against other animals, and with food, water, and medical care always available than they would be if running free. Average citizens, however, are likely to be appalled by pictures showing thousands of animals packed tightly together. They are also likely to think about the social and psychological needs of animals as well as their physical condition. Thus, in some states and in some other countries, laws against certain practices are being passed by public demand. Studies have shown that many consumers are willing to outlaw these practices even if it means higher food costs.

Animal welfare advocates are fighting for the humane treatment of farm animals, and this is a goal most people endorse. The conflict comes over the issue of which practices are inhumane. Not all practices opposed by activists are the result of factory farming; some—for example, the castration of young males without anesthetic—have been used on family farms for generations. As far back as World War II, laying hens were sometimes kept in individual "battery" cages by people who raised only a few chickens in their backyards. But modern city dwellers have no experience with farm animals and tend to view as "inhumane" anything they would not do to their pets.

In 2000 the legislature of New Jersey passed a law directing the state Department of Agriculture to issue regulations ensuring the humane treatment of farm animals. When these regulations appeared, animal activists were dismayed by some of what they contained. The worst aspect, in their view, was that all "routine" or "commonly used" practices taught in veterinary schools were authorized. In the opinion of the activists this defeated the purpose of the law, since many practices to which they object are routine. A coalition of animal welfare organizations filed suit in the hope of getting the regulations struck down or amended.

The Superior Court of New Jersey ruled against the appellants, who then took the case to the New Jersey Supreme Court. That court, after careful consideration of the arguments, overturned the lower court's decision with respect to portions of the regulations. Among other things, it held that just because it is taught in veterinary schools does not necessarily mean that a practice is humane. This decision, though legally applicable only to New Jersey, was hailed as a victory for farm animals everywhere.

The Court's Opinion: Anticruelty Regulations Cannot Exempt Agricultural Practices on Grounds That They Are Routine

Helen Hoens

Helen Hoens has been a justice of the New Jersey Supreme Court since 2006. The following is a portion of her opinion in New Jersey Society for the Prevention of Cruelty to Animals et al. v. New Jersey Department of Agriculture *(2008). In this case, a group of animal welfare organizations challenged regulations issued by New Jersey's Agriculture Department on the grounds that these rules did not fulfill the intent of the state legislature, which had instructed it to ensure that the treatment of farm animals was humane. In particular, the animal advocates objected to the blanket authorization of all farm practices that were routine and were taught in veterinary schools. The court agreed that this was not a valid criterion for determining that a practice is humane and overruled that portion of the regulations. Objections were also raised to a number of specific procedures that the regulations allowed (not all of which are discussed in the excerpt included here). The court decided that because no standards were set for determining whether these procedures*

Helen Hoens, opinion, *New Jersey Society for the Prevention of Cruelty to Animals et al. v. New Jersey Department of Agriculture*, Supreme Court of New Jersey, July 30, 2008.

were performed in a humane way, the regulations could not give blanket permission for their use; but it did not ban them entirely.

In 1996, with little discernable fanfare, the [New Jersey] Legislature enacted a new section of the existing statute regulating animal cruelty. Although that statute, since at least 1898, had essentially left animal welfare and the protection of animals to the New Jersey Society for the Prevention of Cruelty to Animals ("NJSPCA") and its related county organizations, the Legislature decreed that the Department of Agriculture ("the Department") would be vested with certain authority relating to the care and welfare of domestic livestock, commonly referred to as farm animals.

In doing so, the Legislature directed the Department to create and promulgate regulations that would set standards governing the raising, keeping, and marketing of domestic livestock, but it specified that the guiding principle to be utilized in establishing those standards was to be whether the treatment of these animals was "humane." . . .

The dispute before this Court has nothing to do with anyone's love for animals, or with the way in which any of us treats our pets; rather, it requires a balancing of the interests of people and organizations who would zealously safeguard the well-being of all animals, including those born and bred for eventual slaughter, with the equally significant interests of those who make their living in animal husbandry and who contribute, through their effort, to our food supply.

In the end, our focus is not upon, nor would it be appropriate for us to address, whether we deem any of the specifically challenged practices to be, objectively, humane. To engage in that debate would suggest that we have some better understanding of the complex scientific and technical issues than we possibly could have, or that we are in some sense better able to evaluate the extensive record compiled by the Department than is that body itself. . . .

Notwithstanding all of the foregoing, our review of the record compels us to conclude that in its wholesale embrace of the regulations adopted by the Department, the Appellate Division erred. Because we find in those regulations both unworkable standards and an unacceptable delegation of authority to an ill-defined category of presumed experts, we conclude that the Department failed, in part, to carry out its mandate. We therefore conclude that some, but not all, of the regulations are invalid and we reverse only those aspects of the Appellate Division's judgment that concluded otherwise. . . .

Arguments of the Petitioners

Petitioners are a variety of entities, including the NJSPCA, and individuals which describe themselves collectively as "a wide coalition of animal protection organizations, consumers, farmers, and concerned citizens." . . .

As part of the appeal, petitioners asserted that the regulations violated the directive of the Legislature as set forth in the statute itself. More particularly, petitioners contended that in adopting the statute, the Legislature expressed an intention to elevate the treatment of farm animals so as to permit only those practices, procedures, and techniques that meet the definition of "humane." As such, petitioners argued that the regulations fell short of that mandate in several particulars. First, petitioners argued that several subsections of the regulations include a broadly-worded exemption for any practice that meets the definition of a "routine husbandry practice" and that the definition as adopted is both impermissibly vague and not grounded on any evidence in the record. Second, petitioners asserted that some of the subsections included vague or undefined terms and failed to create enforceable standards. Third, petitioners asserted that the regulations authorized a variety of specific practices that do not meet the Department's definition of "humane" and are not in fact humane.

In defending the regulations before the Appellate Division, the Department argued that they were consistent with both the intent and the spirit of the statute and supported by ample scientific evidence. In part, the Department argued that its statutory mandate required it to meet two public policy objectives, namely, preventing cruelty to animals and promoting the continuation of sustainable agriculture in New Jersey. The Department defended its election of "routine husbandry practices" as an appropriate criterion for its safe harbor exemption, explained how the regulations established objectively enforceable standards, and argued that none of the specific practices that petitioners challenged is in fact inhumane.

The Appellate Division, in an unpublished opinion, rejected each of petitioners' challenges and sustained all of the challenged regulations. . . .

Petitioners argue before this Court that the Appellate Division erred in its analysis and failed to recognize that the regulations authorize the continuation, as humane, of practices that are not. Asserting that the statute itself is remedial legislation entitled to be broadly read, petitioners argue that the Appellate Division failed to recognize the particular legislative purpose in utilizing the "humane" standard. According to petitioners, that standard was used by the Legislature to avoid simply allowing the continuation of practices that are merely routine or common. They assert that the Legislature intended instead to require the Department to consider separately whether any particular practice, even if commonly or routinely utilized, is in fact humane. Petitioners urge us to conclude that although the Department recognized this mandate, as evidenced by the definition of humane that it adopted, its regulations fall short by ignoring that definition and by effectively doing precisely what the Legislature sought to avoid. . . .

Petitioners also reiterate the other arguments that they pressed before the Appellate Division. They urge the Court to conclude that the regulations fail to set an enforceable standard by utilizing language, such as "minimize pain," without further definition, so as to provide insufficient guidance to those charged with enforcement and that the regulations therefore fail to establish any standard. Finally, they point to a large number of particular practices that are permitted to be performed by the regulations but that, they assert, are not humane in accordance with the Department's definition or which are of dubious benefit according to the scientific evidence. In short, because the regulations have both specific shortcomings and general ones, petitioners urge this Court to invalidate the regulations in their entirety.

The Department urges this Court to affirm the Appellate Division's carefully analyzed and lengthy opinion and to uphold the regulations both in general and in all of their particulars. . . .

Response of the Agriculture Department

The Department argues in particular that its "routine husbandry practices" exemption is consistent with the statutory mandate and is an appropriate means to permit the continuation of practices that should be permitted. It points out that in response to criticism that its original definition of "routine husbandry practices" was too broad, it introduced and adopted the amended definition, limiting such practices only to those that are "commonly taught" at veterinary schools, land grant colleges, and universities or by agricultural extension agents. . . .

Petitioners first assert that the regulations, in their entirety, fail to carry out the fundamental goal of the Legislature to have the Department create regulations that embody standards that are humane. . . .

More to the point, petitioners point out that the Department itself adopted a definition of humane that many of the practices that are explicitly permitted or that fall within the safe harbor cannot meet. Although they point to several particular practices that they argue are examples of the way in which the regulations fall short, petitioners insist that this defect is so pervasive that the regulations cannot be sustained at all.

Regardless of one's personal view of the overall regulatory scheme or of domestic livestock management in general, the regulations as a whole are consistent with the meaning of the term "humane." In so concluding, we are guided by two considerations. First, petitioners suggest that they have merely pointed to specific examples of treatment that they have identified as falling short of the definition of "humane," in an effort to illustrate a larger defect in the regulations. They argue that these examples alone should suffice to prove the bankruptcy of the process used by the Department in adopting the regulations and should therefore support a decision to invalidate the regulations in their entirety.

We, however, do not agree. Rather, we interpret petitioners' failure to suggest that the great majority of the practices permitted in these apparently uncontroversial requirements are not humane, as significant. That failure is instead evidence that they are not so wide of that mark that they constitute an agency action with which we should interfere. Although one or another of the specifically challenged practices within the regulations may individually fall short of the standard of review that we employ, that is an insufficient ground on which to invalidate the whole. . . .

Authorization of Routine Practices

Petitioners next challenge the inclusion in the regulations of language creating a safe harbor for any act or technique that meets the definition of "routine husbandry practices." This exception, included in one of the subsections of each subchapter, essentially authorizes the use of any and all techniques that meet this definition because it identifies this class of practices as not being prohibited.

The phrase "routine husbandry practices" is among the terms that the Department included in its section on definitions as follows:

> "Routine husbandry practices" means those techniques commonly taught by veterinary schools, land grant colleges, and agricultural extension agents for the benefit of animals, the livestock industry, animal handlers and the public health and which are employed to raise, keep, care, treat, market and transport livestock, including, but not limited to, techniques involved with physical restraint; animal handling; animal identification; animal training; manure management; restricted feeding; restricted watering; restricted exercising; animal housing techniques; reproductive techniques; implantation; vaccination; and use of fencing materials, as long as all other State and Federal laws governing these practices are followed.

Petitioners assert that the definition of "routine husbandry practices" is so broad and all-encompassing that it amounts to an improper delegation of the agency's authority, contrary to its legislative mandate. Moreover, they argue that the record reveals that the Department, in adopting this definition and this standard for what constitutes "humane," failed to even review or evaluate the practices that it would permit. . . .

Amicus [Friend of the court, Bernard] Rollin concurs, arguing that merely because a practice is routinely employed or taught, even if taught at a veterinary school, does not mean that it is humane. Rather, he argues that many practices taught at these institutions are motivated by concerns about the economics of agriculture, focusing on productivity alone, and ignoring any concerns about the welfare of the animals involved. As such, he argues that these practices, even if commonly taught, simply cannot be equated with practices or techniques that are also humane. . . .

Notwithstanding its insistence that its review was careful prior to its decision to effectively place into the hands of this wide-ranging and ill-defined group of presumed experts the power to determine what is humane, there is no evidence in the record that the Department undertook any review, organized or passing, of what these institutions actually teach. . . .

Nor is there any evidence that the Department considered whether the techniques taught in these institutions, whatever those techniques might be, rest in any way on a concern about what practices are humane or have any focus other than expedience or maximization of productivity. Contrary to the Department's assertion, there is no evidence that it considered the intersection between the interests of those who attend these institutions or are taught by them and those who are concerned with the welfare of the animals.

Our review of this aspect of the appeal leads us to conclude that this part of the safe harbor exemption demonstrates two separate flaws. First, it cannot be denied that in enacting this statute, the Legislature directed the Department to achieve a specific goal and that it chose to do so in language that differed from similar statutes in other states. It is significant that the Legislature sought to exempt only "humane" practices from prosecution under the cruelty code. Whereas other states have exempted routine, common, or accepted practices from their cruelty codes, our Legislature chose not to use that language, selecting a different course. . . .

Second, in light of the direct mandate to the Department to adopt regulations that establish practices that are humane, the decision by that agency to authorize an exemption, and therefore to embrace wholesale any technique as long as it is "commonly taught" at any of these institutions, under the circumstances, is an impermissible subdelegation. . . .

Our analysis of petitioners' objections to the several subsections of the regulations that create a safe harbor by reliance on "routine husbandry practices" compels us to conclude that these objections have merit. By adopting a definition of exceptional breadth, by failing to create an adequate record in support of this decision, and by implicitly permitting techniques that cannot meet the statutory mandate to base its regulations on a determination about what is humane, the Department has adopted regulations that are arbitrary and capricious. We therefore strike as invalid the definition of "routine husbandry practices," and that part of each of the subsections of the regulations referring thereto.

Tail Docking of Dairy Cows

Petitioners also challenged individually a number of practices that are specifically permitted by the regulations, asserting that they are demonstrably inhumane and that the Department's authorization thereof is unsupported by sound science. In particular, petitioners point to several procedures utilized by some farming operations that are physically painful and, they contend, are emotionally distressing to the animals. At the same time, they argue, these same practices cannot be justified because they are often of little or no value. In response, the Department counters that there is ample scientific evidence in the record that supports the continued use of each of these procedures. Moreover, the Department asserts that because the regulations include limits on the manner and circumstances in which any of these disputed practices is permitted, the practical result is that each of them is only performed in a humane manner. . . .

The first specific practice that petitioners attack relates only to dairy cattle. This practice, known as "tail docking," is a procedure that involves "the amputation of the lower portion of a dairy cow's tail." (Lawrence J. Hutchinson). Petitioners contend that tail docking cannot meet the Department's definition of humane, and they point to evidence of a consensus among scientists that tail docking is without any "apparent animal health, welfare, or human health justification." (C.L. Stull et al.)

They further assert that tail docking causes acute pain and interferes with the ability of the affected animals to perform natural behaviors, including flicking their tails to chase away flies in the summer.... Petitioners argue that a practice from which the animal derives no benefit, and that will cause it to suffer distress, cannot be humane.

The Department contends that, despite the AVMA's [American Veterinary Medical Association] position paper, its decision to permit tail docking to continue to be performed complied with its statutory mandate to create humane standards. The agency points out that it responded to comments objecting to the practice, and that it reasoned that the practice should be permitted because it may lead to better milk quality and udder health, and it may also reduce the spread of diseases....

Although we recognize the considerable expertise that the Department brought to bear in reaching its decision to include tail docking within its list of permitted practices, it is difficult to find in this record any support for this particular practice, and none that meets the requisite standard of our review. The record amply demonstrates that, far from being humane, this practice is specifically disparaged by both the AVMA and the CVMA [Canadian Veterinary Medical Association] as having no benefit and as leading to distress. The only scientific evidence that even suggests that the practice might have some possible benefit is inconclusive at best.

More to the point, the record in support of the practice is so weak that even the industry trade group, like the Department, "discourages" it, leaving it apparently to the individual conscience of each dairy farmer....

Apart from failing to adhere to the Legislative mandate that the agency permit only those practices that it finds to be humane (as opposed to not inhumane), because this practice finds no support at all in the record, to the extent that the regulation permits it, that aspect of the regulation is both arbitrary and capricious. In the absence of evidence in the record to support the practice or to confine it to circumstances in which it has a benefit and is performed in a manner that meets an objective definition of humane, this aspect of the regulation cannot stand.

Painful Procedures

For purposes of our analysis, we have identified several of the challenged practices that we find it appropriate to consider together. This group comprises three specific practices that are similar in terms of petitioners' focus and our evaluation of the record: (1) castration of swine, horses, and calves, (2) debeaking of chickens and turkeys, and (3) toe-trimming of turkeys. Each is a procedure that petitioners assert is, by and large, unnecessary, because each seeks to prevent behaviors, or the effects thereof, in which animals would likely not engage were they not raised in close quarters. In addition, petitioners challenge these practices because each is performed without anesthetics, thus causing the animals significant, if not severe, pain. . . .

The record reflects that there is evidence that demonstrates these practices confer a benefit on the animals in light of their living conditions. For example, castration is generally employed to reduce aggression between male animals, including horses and cattle, when they are kept together in a herd. Similarly, beak trimming is used to reduce such behaviors as cannibalism and pecking within a flock. In a like manner, toe-trimming is performed to prevent turkeys from climbing on one another and causing injury and to prevent them from inflicting injury on their caregivers or handlers. Although there are other management techniques that might achieve the desired results without employing these particular methods, there is sufficient credible evidence in the record to support the agency's conclusion that these techniques can be performed in a humane manner and should be permitted.

Were the issue before this Court merely a matter of deciding whether the scientific evidence supports the use of the procedures at all, our task would be a simple one; were that our task, we would be constrained to conclude that there is sufficient evidence in the record to support the Department's decision that they be permitted. That, however, is not the only question before this Court. Instead, the question is whether there is sufficient support in the record for the Department's decision to specifically permit these practices in the context of its mandate that it adopt regulations that will ensure that the treatment of animals is humane. . . .

The limitation that the agency asserts is the lynchpin of ensuring that these procedures are performed in a humane manner cannot pass muster. The regulations do not define the terms "sanitary manner," "knowledgeable individual," or "minimize pain," nor is there any objective criteria against which to determine whether any particular individual performing the procedure measures up to these standards. As a result, the regulations that the Department suggests will ensure that the procedures will be accomplished in a humane manner provide no standard against which to test that they are in fact so performed. . . .

Similarly, without any standard as to what the regulation means in terms of minimizing pain, there is no standard at all. . . .

By including these practices in the subsections of the regulations that authorize them to be performed, the Department has created an unworkable enforcement scheme. That is to say, there is no standard against which to judge whether a particular individual is "knowledgeable" or whether a method is "sanitary" in the context of an agricultural setting or whether the manner in which the procedure is being performed constitutes a "way as to minimize pain." That being the case, we are constrained to conclude that these aspects of the regulations fail to fix a standard that will ensure that the practices are in fact humane and, at the same time, are too vague to establish a standard that is enforceable. . . .

Our consideration of the issues raised in this appeal and our review of the record have led us to conclude that certain aspects of these regulations cannot be sustained. We do not intend, however, to suggest that the defects in the regulations are pervasive or that all of the many practices that the Department specifically considered and permitted cannot be performed in a humane manner. To be sure, we have concluded that the "routine husbandry practices" and the "knowledgeable individual and in such a way as to minimize pain" safe harbors cannot be sustained as written, but neither of these determinations effects a ban on any of the particular practices. Rather, any practice, technique, or procedure not otherwise prohibited by the regulations may be utilized by any farmer, risking only that the practice, technique, or procedure will be challenged by an appropriate enforcement authority as inhumane. . . .

Our decision, therefore, should not be understood to be a ban on the continuation of any specific practice, but merely a recognition that some of the standards that purport to define them so as to ensure that they are actually performed in a manner that meets the statute's command that all such practices be humane have fallen short.

| "There has been a growing concern among the public, government leaders, and even industry groups regarding the humane treatment of farmed animals."

Many Agricultural Practices Are Cruel to Animals and Should Be Banned

Erin M. Tobin and Katherine A. Meyer

Erin M. Tobin and Katherine A. Meyer are attorneys for the coalition of animal welfare organizations that brought suit in New Jersey Society for the Prevention of Cruelty to Animals et al. v. New Jersey Department of Agriculture. The following viewpoint consists of excerpts from the brief they filed when they first submitted the case to the Superior Court of New Jersey (it was later appealed to the New Jersey Supreme Court). In the brief they explain why animal welfare advocates opposed the regulations issued by the Department of Agriculture (DOA) for the treatment of farm animals. The New Jersey legislature had instructed the DOA to ensure that farming practices were humane, but the DOA exempted "routine" procedures from regulation. In the brief, the attorneys describe common practices that animal welfare advocates believe are not humane (the original descriptions are more detailed than the excerpts included here). They conclude that the regulations violate the law and should not be allowed to stand.

Erin M. Tobin and Katherine A. Meyer, brief of appellants, *New Jersey Society for the Prevention of Cruelty to Animals et al. v. New Jersey Department of Agriculture*, Superior Court of New Jersey, November 2, 2005.

In the United States and throughout the world, small, family farms are disappearing from the landscape and quickly being supplanted by industrialized mass production systems, or "factory farms." Factory farms seek to maximize profits by producing and confining large numbers of animals in a small amount of space, thus consolidating resources and reducing overhead costs. Unfortunately, this transformation towards large, intensive farming systems has come at significant cost to the welfare of hundreds of millions of farmed animals, who are no longer allowed to enjoy any semblance of normal behavior, but instead are treated as if they were inanimate objects on a factory assembly line.

With few state laws, and no federal laws, governing the treatment of these animals, producers have been free to limit these animals' access to basic life-sustaining necessities, such as sunlight, space, food, and water, in order to reduce producers' costs and increase profit margins.

In response, there has been a growing concern among the public, government leaders, and even industry groups regarding the humane treatment of farmed animals, leading many of these entities to denounce "common" or "routine" agricultural practices on the grounds that they are not humane. For example, the American Veterinary Association ("AVMA"), the United Egg Producers ("UEP"), and the largest fast food restaurants have all condemned the practice of "forced molting" egg-laying hens, a process employed by egg producers that essentially starves hens to induce a second phase of egg production. Florida has banned the common practice of confining pregnant pigs in individual crates that are barely wider than the animals themselves—a practice that prevents them from performing basic, natural behaviors such as walking or turning around. In addition, the AVMA recently voted to oppose the common practice of docking the tails of dairy cattle, because it "provides no benefit to the animal." ...

Thus, members of the public, the scientific community, and governments around the world have all recognized a need to reform existing inhumane agricultural practices.

New Jersey's Mandate

In 1996, the New Jersey Legislature enacted legislation directing the State Board of Agriculture and the Department of Agriculture [DOA] to develop and adopt standards for the "humane" raising, keeping, care, treatment, marketing and sale of domestic livestock, and to develop "rules and regulations governing the enforcement of those standards." This landmark legislation marked the first time that a state would establish specific standards governing the humane treatment of domestic livestock. . . .

DOA asserted that the standards were intended to "serve as the baseline for determining inhumane treatment" of domestic livestock, and would ensure that "any act or treatment that falls below these standards can be *accurately identified and swiftly addressed by all applicable law enforcement entities.*" However, for each species covered by the "standards," the proposed regulations included a broad exemption for any "routine husbandry practices."

In response, DOA received over 6,500 comments—the overwhelming majority of which expressed strong opposition to the draft regulations for permitting numerous routine factory farming practices that are clearly inhumane. Citizens and organizations—including individuals, scientists, local Societies for the Prevention of Cruelty to Animals, organic farmers, and grass-roots organizations, as well as nearly every national animal protection organization in the United States—expressed significant concern with the proposed standards, largely on the ground that they authorized numerous cruel and inhumane practices, simply because those practices are already "routinely" employed by animal producers. These practices include starving egg-laying hens to force them into producing more eggs, confining calves raised for veal and pregnant pigs in crates so small that they cannot turn around, painfully mutilating animals without anesthesia, and subjecting animals who are emaciated or cannot walk on their own to the rigors of transportation to slaughter houses.

Commenters also criticized the proposed regulations' because, in many instances, they failed to set meaningful standards that law enforcement agents, such as the New Jersey SPCA [Society for the Prevention of Cruelty to Animals], can enforce. . . .

The Legislature directed DOA to develop and adopt standards for the "humane" raising, keeping, care, treatment, marketing, and sale of domestic livestock. DOA itself has defined the term "humane" to mean "marked by compassion, sympathy, and consideration for the welfare of animals," which, according to DOA, encompasses the *physical or psychological harmony between the animal and its surroundings, characterized by the absence of deprivation, aversive stimulation, over stimulation or any other imposed condition that adversely affects health* and productivity of the animal."

Nevertheless, rather than devise standards that would eliminate inhumane practices, the final regulations codify numerous existing factory farming practices that the Record overwhelmingly demonstrates cause severe hunger, pain, stress, disease, and even mortality in animals. Therefore, there is no rational basis for concluding that these practices reflect the "compassion," "sympathy," or "consideration" for the "welfare of animals," that DOA is obligated to ensure. Accordingly, the regulations are unlawful and must be set aside.

The Practice of "Forced Molting"

The practice of "forced molting" egg-laying hens—whereby hens are *intentionally starved* for 5 to 14 days in order to shock their systems into an unnatural egg-laying cycle—causes these animals severe hunger, stress, disease, and even death, and is opposed by national veterinary associations, industry groups, and even fast food restaurants. Nevertheless, DOA's regulations expressly allow producers to starve egg-laying hens by providing that, for up to 14 days, "*[f]eed may be withdrawn from adult poultry* during an induced molt."

In light of the consensus that forced molting through starvation should be prohibited, DOA's conclusion that this practice is nevertheless "humane," is clearly arbitrary and capricious. . . .

Furthermore, starving animals to the point that they lose up to 30 percent of their body weight, and causing individual animals to die as a result—as permitted by DOA's regulations—is precisely the type of conduct that is deemed "cruel" when applied in other contexts. . . .

DOA attempts to justify this regulation on the grounds that forced molting is a "*recognized agricultural industry practice.*" However, whether a practice is a "recognized agricultural industry practice" or not is simply not relevant to whether the practice is "humane"—the overarching requirement imposed by the Legislature. . . .

Confining Animals

DOA's regulations also fail to set "humane" standards with respect to several species that are routinely subjected to grossly restrictive confinement systems. In particular, the regulations allow producers to house calves raised for veal and pregnant pigs (or "sows") in crates barely wider than the animals themselves, which prevent the animals from performing basic, natural movements, such as even *turning around*. However, studies in the Record show that such conditions cause animals severe pain and suffering. Accordingly, the regulations are both inconsistent with [the law] and arbitrary and capricious.

The regulations' provisions concerning the raising of veal calves—which were taken *verbatim* from the veal industry's own guide for the production of veal—allow calves to be tethered and housed for the bulk of their lives in crates so small that the animals *cannot even turn around*. However, evidence in the Record overwhelmingly demonstrates that such conditions seriously jeopardize calf welfare—compromising calf immune systems, causing "stereoptypies" [repeated sequences of movement without purpose] and other abnormal behaviors, and increasing disease and mortality. In light of these severe health effects, DOA's regulations are not "humane," in contravention of the Legislature's direction. . . .

The regulations also expressly allow pork producers to confine pregnant pigs in stalls—or "gestation crates"—that are barely wider than the animals themselves, and prevent pigs from exercising or performing even the most basic, natural movements, such as simply turning around. However, the practice of raising sows for most of their reproductive lives in this manner has been shown to cause sows a host of physical and psychological ailments. Therefore, the practice of confining pregnant sows in gestation crates is without *any* "compassion, sympathy or consideration for the welfare of animals."

Substantial evidence in the Record demonstrates that confining pregnant pigs in gestation crates for the bulk of their reproductive lives, *i.e.*, three to five years, and denying them the ability to move naturally or turn around in their crates, causes numerous physical and psychological health problems, including decreased muscle mass and bone strength and cardiovascular disease, as well as boredom, apathy, and stereotypic behavior. . . .

Moreover, in a landmark British case, the court found that McDonald's Corporation was accurately accused of "cruel practices" by animal welfare activists, because pork used and sold by McDonald's originated from producers that confined pregnant sows in gestation crates that deprived the animals of any "freedom of movement." . . .

Mutilating Livestock

DOA's regulations also expressly permit practices that painfully and needlessly mutilate livestock. The practices discussed below—including "tail docking," "castrating," "de-beaking," and "de-toeing" animals *without the use of anesthesia*—cause animals acute and chronic pain. For these reasons, DOA's approval of industry practices that cruelly mutilate livestock—without any limitations on how or when these practices are conducted—is patently *not* "humane" or "marked by compassion, sympathy, and consideration for the welfare of animals." as required by the agency's own definition of the term.

"Tail docking" is the procedure by which producers amputate the lower portion of a dairy cow's tail. Although DOA attempts to justify this practice as necessary to improve cow hygiene and milk quality, the overwhelming consensus among scientists is that it is without *any* "apparent animal health, welfare, or human health justifications." (C.L. Stull) Thus, the practice is not "humane" by any definition of the term.

The Record amply demonstrates that tail docking causes acute pain and interferes with the animals' ability to perform natural behaviors. . . .

DOA's regulations expressly permit the practice of castrating animals, including cattle, horses, and swine, without anesthesia, despite the fact that the Record shows that this causes livestock significant pain. For this reason, the regulation cannot possibly be deemed "humane."

Indeed, as the Record overwhelmingly demonstrates, castrating animals without anesthesia can be devastatingly painful. . . .

The primary justification for castration is that it reduces aggression in male animals. However, in most cases, the procedure is not even *necessary* to accomplish this objective. (Castration "is not necessary if animals are slaughtered before these maturational changes occur").

Moreover, as the Record also demonstrates, the painful effects of castration can be significantly reduced by the use of anesthesia, or, at the very least, by limiting the age of the animal experiencing the procedure. . . .

DOA's regulations also permit the practice of removing part of the beaks of chickens and turkeys—to reduce pecking caused when birds are kept in overcrowded conditions—with a hot blade (otherwise known as "de-beaking" or "beak-trimming"), limitations that would prevent birds from feeling this painful procedure.

Overwhelming evidence in the Record shows that the practice of removing a bird's beak with a metal blade causes "short-term" and "chronic" pain as well as "acute stress." . . .

Moreover, the Record shows that providing birds more space, and also breeding birds to be less aggressive, reduces the incidence of excessive pecking. . . .

DOA's regulations also explicitly permit the practice of "toe trimming," or "de-toeing," whereby producers amputate the toes of turkeys to reduce the animals' ability to scratch handlers. However, Record evidence shows that toe trimming causes animals acute pain. . . .

Requirements on Mutilations

DOA asserts that the regulations authorizing mutilations nevertheless establish "humane" standards because they also require that these practices be performed in such a way as to "minimize pain." However, the phrase "minimize pain" does not establish any meaningful standard by which the regulated community, enforcement agents, or the courts can determine whether conduct actually complies with this standard, and, hence, the regulations also fail to meet DOA's own stated objective of setting "baseline" standards that will allow law enforcement to *accurately identif[y] and swiftly address[]*" inhumane practices. Regulations with similarly vague language have been declared unlawful.

For example, DOA's regulations vaguely permit "branding" of cattle as long as it is "performed in a sanitary manner by a knowledgeable individual and *in such a way as to minimize pain.*" Under the plain language of the regulation, DOA appears to permit *any* type of branding—despite the fact that some forms of branding are much more painful than others. Thus, instead of prohibiting those forms of branding that are inherently more painful than others, the regulations would permit *all* forms of branding as long as each is done in a manner that "minimizes pain"—with absolutely no guidance as to what this means. . . .

Transporting Emaciated and Downed Animals

DOA's regulations also authorize producers to transport emaciated and "downed" animals—*i.e.*, animals who are unable to stand up or walk on their own—even though the process of loading these animals onto transport trucks is inherently, and significantly, painful. As numerous animal welfare organizations and experts explained in the Record, such animals should instead be humanely euthanized to reduce their suffering.

It is patently arbitrary for DOA to *permit* the transport of emaciated and "downed" animals to slaughter when, at the same time, DOA recognizes that it is *not* "humane" to transport such animals to market (from where they are then sold for slaughter). . . .

DOA concedes that *emaciated* animals "are likely not strong enough to withstand the stresses of transport," but, nevertheless, allows them to be transported to slaughter facilities because the agency believes it is "appropriate to provide *some flexibility to owners on where and when slaughter may take place.*" However, providing "flexibility" to producers was not the purpose of these statutorily-mandated regulations; rather, DOA was instructed to set "humane" standards for livestock, and neither the statute, nor DOA's regulations, define "humane" to encompass owner "flexibility." ...

"Routine Husbandry Practices"

In addition to the practices that are expressly *permitted* by DOA's regulations, under the regulations, agricultural practices that are not expressly *prohibited*, are also permitted as long as they are considered "routine husbandry practices." DOA defines this term to mean those techniques "commonly taught by veterinary schools, land grant colleges, and agricultural extension agents."

However, by creating a vast exemption for practices, regardless of whether they are "humane," the regulations are flatly inconsistent with the Legislature's mandate. As further demonstrated below, the regulations are also arbitrary and capricious because the "routine husbandry practices" exception fails to set a meaningful "standard" to inform enforcement agents, the public, or the courts of precisely what conduct is prohibited, and because, in fact, there are many such practices that are clearly *not* "humane."

Because the plain terms of the enabling legislation direct *DOA* to "develop" humane standards, the agency may not shirk its regulatory responsibility by crafting a vast exception for any practices that are taught by "veterinary schools, land grant colleges, and agricultural extensions," irrespective of whether such practices are even *known* to DOA, and regardless of whether such practices are "humane."

If the New Jersey Legislature had wanted to exempt "routine husbandry practices" from the reach of the State's animal cruelty statute it could clearly have amended the statute to accomplish this result. In fact, several State cruelty codes contain such an exemption. ...

By crafting a broad exemption from the cruelty code for *any* "routine" husbandry practices "commonly" taught by "veterinary schools, land grant colleges, and agricultural extension

115

agents," DOA has also failed to "develop" a "standard" for the humane treatment of animals, as required by the enabling legislation. Indeed, because the exemption applies to any practice "commonly taught" by these institutions, without any apparent geographic limitation, the regulations seemingly allow any practice that is "commonly taught" by *any* such entity anywhere in the country or even the world. However, as the Record demonstrates, there are hundreds of veterinary schools, land grant colleges, and agriculture extensions throughout *this* country that teach a wide variety of practices at their institutions. Yet, the regulations arbitrarily provide no guidance whatsoever as to how enforcement agents should determine whether a practice is "commonly" taught. . . .

Exemption Permits Inhumane Practices

DOA's exemption for "routine husbandry practices" also authorizes numerous farming practices that simply are not "humane." Indeed, each of the practices discussed in the preceding section of this brief, such as forced molting, castration without anesthesia, and tail docking—which are all clearly not "humane"—are routinely taught at "veterinary schools, land grant colleges, and agricultural extensions." Moreover, the Record demonstrates that many other practices that will be permitted under the regulations as "routine husbandry practices" are also not "humane."

The practice of feeding ducks and geese by force for the production of "*pate de foie gras*" is permitted under the new regulations as a "routine husbandry practice," because it is not specifically addressed by the regulations. However, the production of *foie gras* involves force feeding ducks and geese by placing a long tube down the birds' throats and pumping food directly into their stomachs, causing their livers to become diseased and swollen. Because the Record undeniably demonstrates that this practice causes birds significant pain and suffering, DOA's authorization of this "routine" practice violates the Legislature's mandate. . . .

DOA's exception also authorizes the use of intensive genetic selection to breed larger, fast-growing "broiler" chickens and turkeys, as well as more productive egg-laying hens, to maximize meat and egg production, because this practice is also "commonly taught" by agricultural institutions. However, substantial evidence in the Record demonstrates that fast-growing strains of chickens and turkeys suffer chronic pain from skeletal deformities, muscle disease, and cardio-pulmonary disease, increased susceptibility to painful contact dermatitis, reduced immune function, and increased mortality compared to slow growing strains. Given this evidence and the availability of slower growing strains that do not experience these health and welfare problems, this practice is clearly not "humane." . . .

In response to Appellants' concerns about this practice, DOA referenced a provision in the regulations that requires that "poultry shall be provided sufficient and nutritious feed to allow for growth and maintenance of adequate body condition," as a basis for not developing a specific standard governing this practice. However, that provision of the regulations does *not* apply to breeding practices, and does not prevent producers from breeding birds used for meat production, birds used to breed these birds, and birds used for egg production, in such a way that they experience significant health and welfare problems. . . .

In short, it is readily apparent that, instead of developing standards based on an independent determination that specific agricultural practices are "humane," DOA has chosen to codify agricultural practices that are currently in use, *regardless* of whether they are humane. The agency's failure to abide by the Legislature's mandate is clear from the Record, which shows that, in defending practices proven to be inhumane,

DOA repeatedly resorts to the fact that a practice is a "recognized agricultural industry practice." In addition, rather than develop "humane" standards, DOA has also created a vast exemption for "routine husbandry practices" taught by any veterinary schools, land grant colleges, or agricultural extensions anywhere in the world, even though many of these institutions teach practices that are blatantly cruel and not "humane." Moreover, DOA's regulations make it nearly impossible for law enforcement entities, including the New Jersey SPCA, to carry out their statutory obligations to enforce the state's animal cruelty laws.

> "[Animal welfare advocates] don't demonize meat . . . or the people who produce it. Instead, they use softer rhetoric, focusing on a campaign even committed carnivores can get behind: better conditions for farm animals."

Support for Humane Treatment of Farm Animals Is Growing

Kim Severson

Kim Severson is a staff writer for The New York Times, *focusing on food and cultural trends. She is also the author of several cookbooks. In the following article, written at the time the New Jersey Supreme Court agreed to review* New Jersey Society for the Prevention of Cruelty to Animals et al. v. New Jersey Department of Agriculture, *she describes recent trends in the animal welfare movement, featuring the founder of Farm Sanctuary, which led the coalition that brought the suit. She explains that although animal rights activists believe people should be vegetarians and stop using animals for any purpose, they have found that they can gain respect and influence only through a less radical agenda. They now join forces with animal welfare advocates in working toward better conditions for farm animals, using tactics such as organizing political campaigns and buying stock in major food corporations. Some such corporations are becoming interested in animal welfare, not because of activism but because it is now supported by consumers.*

The first farm animal Gene Baur ever snatched from a stockyard was a lamb he named Hilda.

That was 1986. She's now buried under a little tombstone near the center of Farm Sanctuary, 180 acres of vegan nirvana here in the Finger Lakes region of upstate New York.

Back then, Mr. Baur was living in a school bus near a tofu factory in Pennsylvania and selling vegetarian hot dogs at Grateful Dead concerts to support his animal rescue operation.

Now, more than a thousand animals once destined for the slaughterhouse live here and on another Farm Sanctuary property in California. Farm Sanctuary has a $5.7 million budget, fed in part by a donor club named after his beloved Hilda. Supporters can sign up for a Farm Sanctuary MasterCard. A $200-a-seat gala dinner in Los Angeles this fall will feature seitan Wellington and stars like Emily Deschanel and Forest Whitaker.

As Farm Sanctuary has grown, so too has its influence. Soon, due in part to the organization's work, veal calves and pregnant pigs in Arizona won't be kept in cages so tight they can't turn around. Eggs from cage-free hens have become so popular that there is a national shortage. A law in Chicago bans the sale of foie gras.

And earlier this month, the New Jersey Supreme Court agreed to hear a case concerning common farming practices that a coalition led by Farm Sanctuary says are inhumane.

All of these developments reflect the maturation and sophistication of Mr. Baur and others in a network of animal activists who have more control over America's dinner table than ever before.

Among animal rights groups, the 1980s were considered the decade of grass-roots activism. The 1990s saw the rise of court actions and ballot initiatives. This decade is about building budgets, influencing policy and cultivating elected officials, all with a deliberate focus on livestock.

Farm Sanctuary and other groups still know how to make the most of gory slaughterhouse footage from hidden cameras. The animals they call "rescued"—some abandoned, some saved from natural disasters, some left for dead at slaughterhouses—clearly started life as someone else's property.

But in recent years they have adopted more subtle tactics, like holding stock in major food corporations, organizing nimble political campaigns and lobbying lawmakers.

While some groups, like the Animal Welfare Institute, work with ranchers to codify the best methods of raising animals for meat and eggs, most, like Farm Sanctuary and People for the Ethical Treatment of Animals, ultimately want people to stop using even wool and honey because they believe the products exploit living creatures.

But all of these believers have learned that with less stridency comes more respect and influence in food politics. So they no longer concentrate their energy on burning effigies of Colonel Sanders and stealing chickens. They don't demonize meat—with the exception of foie gras and veal—or the people who produce it. Instead, they use softer rhetoric, focusing on a campaign even committed carnivores can get behind: better conditions for farm animals.

In some ways, it's simply a matter of style.

"Instead of telling it like it is, we're learning to present things in a more moderate way," Mr. Baur said. "When it comes to this vegan ideal, that's an aspiration. Would I love everyone to be vegan? Yes. But we want to be respectful and not judgmental."

Interest in Animal Welfare Is Growing

Certainly, concerns over health and food safety, and a growing interest in where food comes from among consumers and chefs, has made animal welfare an easier sell.

Technology has helped savvy activists deliver their message, too—specifically mass e-mail, easily concealed cameras and the ability to quickly distribute images online, like footage of slaughterhouses and the 2004 spoof "The Meatrix."

They have also learned to harness the power of celebrity in a tabloid culture, courting as spokespeople anyone famous who might have recently put down steak tartare in favor of vegetable carpaccio.

"I think there is a shift in public consciousness," said Bruce Friedrich, vice president of international grass-roots campaigns for PETA. "When Cameron Diaz learns that pigs are smarter than 3-year-olds and she's like, 'Oh my God, I'm eating my niece,' that has an impact."

The image makeover has been so successful that a 2006 survey of 5,000 people ages 13 to 24 showed that PETA was the nonprofit organization most would like to volunteer for, according to the market research firm Label Networks. The American Red Cross was second.

Beyond image polishing, animal rights groups also learned how to marshal resources and set up a classic "good-cop, bad-cop" dynamic to put farm animal welfare on legislative agendas. The Chicago foie gras ban was passed because the nation's largest animal rights groups coordinated their strategies, according to several who were involved. A Chicago alderman, Joe Moore, read an article about the fight over foie gras between the chefs Charlie Trotter and Rick Tramonto and proposed a ban. Word spread quickly among local and national animal rights groups, some of whom Mr. Moore invited to play a leading role.

The game was on. Farm Sanctuary put one of its lobbyists on the case. The Humane Society of the United States paid for large ads in the city's newspapers. The activists gave Mr. Moore a controversial video supposedly showing life inside a California foie gras operation made by the Animal Protection and Rescue League and PETA. He screened it at a city hearing.

PETA, whose over-the-top protests are considered divisive by some animal rights groups, stayed away on the day of the vote. The law is now being reconsidered, and PETA has unleashed its supporters.

PETA uses more than half of its $30 million budget to poke the meat and fast-food industry in the eye with shock-based educational campaigns. PETA protesters have handed out Unhappy Meals filled with bloody, dismembered toy animals and miniature KFC buckets filled with packets of fake blood and bones.

As factions in the animal rights movement continue to grow and splinter, sometimes using violence to make their point, the Humane Society, which is 30 years older than PETA, has emerged as the reasonable, wise big brother of the farm animal protection movement.

The arrival of Wayne Pacelle as head of the Humane Society in 2004 both turbo-charged the farm animal welfare movement and gave it a sheen of respectability.

As the organization's first vegan president, he quickly sharpened the group's focus to farm animals. He also absorbed smaller organizations, merging with the 180,000-member Doris Day Animal League and the Fund for Animals. The budget has jumped to $132 million from $75 million, Mr. Pacelle said.

Like PETA, the Humane Society has purchased enough stock in corporations like Tyson, Wal-Mart, McDonald's and Smithfield's to have the legal clout to introduce resolutions.

Mr. Friedrich said PETA had some early success pressuring stockholders when it was fighting to stop companies from testing soap and beauty products on animals. It then began buying stock in McDonald's, attending a shareholder's meeting for the first time in 1998.

Like Mr. Baur, Mr. Pacelle understands that not everyone is going to stop eating animals, so he focuses on what he calls the three R's: refinement of farming techniques, reducing meat consumption and replacement of animal products. That way, he hopes, the Humane Society tent is big enough to include both ardent meat eaters and hard-core vegans.

The broader-umbrella approach is working. Take the case of Wolfgang Puck. In March, he announced that he would stop serving foie gras and buy eggs only from chickens not confined to small cages. Veal, pork and poultry suppliers will have to abide by stricter standards, too.

For five years before the announcement, Mr. Baur's group had been pressuring Mr. Puck to change his meaty ways. Mr. Puck, in an interview in March, said that had nothing to do with his new policies. He simply came to the conclusion that better standards were the best thing for his customers, his food and the animals. But he did credit the Humane Society for his education.

Mr. Puck met Mr. Pacelle through Sharon Patrick, a branding consultant he had hired. Ms. Patrick, the former president of Martha Stewart Living Omnimedia, believed animal welfare could be an important component in her plan for Mr. Puck.

She brokered a meeting between the two men, and eight months later Mr. Puck presented his new animal welfare plan.

But farmers and corporations are only gingerly endorsing animal rights groups—if at all.

The flurry of corporate animal welfare policies that began in 1999 with McDonald's are simply sound corporate strategy, company representatives say. The genesis was likely the 1993 E. coli outbreak at Jack in the Box restaurants, which sickened hundreds and killed four children. Companies realized they had to get a better handle on where their meat was coming from.

And they say it had nothing to do with PETA.

"Ask them and they will tell you they are the sole responsible party for bringing all these changes, but I have yet to see one of their campaigns produce results where they affected the company in terms of customer traffic or profitability," said Denny Lynch, a spokesman for Wendy's.

Like other big fast food companies, Wendy's has been a target of animal activists' campaigns. Earlier this month, it announced a strengthened animal welfare policy.

Burger King executives say that at their company, too, change is driven by consumers, not activist pressure.

"If we think consumers are a little more engaged in this, then so are we," said Steve Grover, vice president for food safety, quality assurance and regulatory compliance. "I look at it like a hockey player. I want to be there before the puck gets there."

Cattle ranchers say pressure from PETA and Farm Sanctuary are not the reason they have started handling animals with more care. As the owners of Niman Ranch and Coleman Natural discovered, people are willing to pay more for meat from animals that are better cared for and whose origins can be traced from birth through processing.

"The groups that don't want us to eat any animals at all are so radical and off-the-wall that we don't even worry about them," said Scott Sell, the owner of Quail Ridge Ag and Livestock Services, a Georgia cattle company. "In our industry we are the original animal welfarists. We take care of the animals because they take care of us."

But Temple Grandin, the animal science expert from Colorado State University who first led McDonald's executives on a tour of their suppliers' slaughterhouses, believes that activists had plenty of impact on changes in how farm animals are cared for.

"Activist pressure starts it because heat softens steel," she said. But she also offered some friendly advice. "What the activists' groups have to be careful about is that you want to soften the steel and not vaporize it."

Activists have only slightly warmer relations with chefs, despite their recent fascination with farming.

For example, Mr. Trotter said animal welfare has become more important because American gastronomic consumers increasingly want to do right by the animals they eat.

"You don't just have to be a card-carrying PETA member anymore to go that route," he said in an e-mail message.

The chefs Mario Batali and Adam Perry Lang, along with the restaurateur Joe Bastianich, are creating a company called BBL Beef Brokers to produce humanely raised meat that is pampered from the farm to the slaughterhouse.

"From the chef's perspective it comes down to, 'Yeah, the steak looks good but why is it not performing?'" Mr. Perry Lang said. "It's because of how the animal was raised and handled. That's not animal rights, but it is animal welfare."

Although animal rights groups and chefs might agree that farm animals need to be treated with more care, one side wants to put those animals on the grill and the other wants to simply hang out with them.

The chasm between the two groups spilled over into the August edition of *VegNews*, a glossy magazine that is a mix of *People* and *Real Simple* for the meatless set. The magazine printed a publisher's note taking the international gastronomic group Slow Food to task for not including more vegetarians. The story carried the headline "The Developmentally Disabled Food Movement" and called the organization's leaders "human-centric food snobs."

Erika Lesser, executive director of Slow Food U.S.A., said that kind of jab keeps the two sides apart.

"There is a place at the Slow Food table for vegetarians, for omnivores, whatever your 'itarian' persuasion is, but I haven't met many vegetarians who are willing to sit at the table with omnivores," she said.

The gap between animal lovers and animal lovers who love to eat them is exactly what Mr. Baur, a man who eats noodles with margarine, soy sauce and brewer's yeast and has only barely heard of Chez Panisse, would like to close.

"We're not really in philosophical alignment," he said. "But I like to think we're in strategic alliance."

"Litigation like the present case in New Jersey diverts citizens and animal activists (at least those really interested in improving conditions for livestock) from supporting farmers committed to taking the best care of their animals."

Farmers and Veterinarians Believe Current Farm Practices Are Humane

Neil D. Hamilton

Neil D. Hamilton is a professor of law, the director of the Agricultural Law Center at Drake University Law School, and chairman of the Agriculture Law Section of the Association of American Law Schools. In the following viewpoint, written before the New Jersey Supreme Court's ruling on New Jersey Society for the Prevention of Cruelty to Animals et al. v. New Jersey Department of Agriculture, *he argues that litigation will not settle the debate between proponents of animal rights and advocates of animal welfare. Animal rights activists want to extend human-based legal "rights" to animals and oppose the consumption of meat, while animal welfare advocates want to ensure the best possible care of animals raised for food. He argues that many of the practices considered inhumane by nonfarmers and consumers are done on family farms as well as "factory farms" and are not considered cruel by farmers or veterinarians. There are better ways to deal with the problem of factory farming than arguing*

Neil D. Hamilton, "One Bad Day: Thoughts on the Difference Between Animal Rights and Animal Welfare," *Michigan Law Review First Impressions*, vol. 106, March 2008, pp. 138–42. Copyright © 2008 by Neil D. Hamilton. Reprinted by permission of the publisher and author.

in court about what is humane, he contends. In Hamilton's opinion it is puzzling that some people apparently find the rights of animals more attractive than those of farmers, eaters, or workers, and he believes that attitudes favoring animals over humans are misguided.

The lawsuit pitting the New Jersey Society for the Prevention of Cruelty to Animals against the New Jersey Department of Agriculture brings into sharp focus the issue of animal rights versus animal welfare that has been dividing animal activists, farmers, and society for decades. On one side are proponents of animal rights—a set of rights articulated by humans but granted to animals to govern how we treat them. For many believers this includes the right not to be owned and certainly not to be eaten. On the other side are proponents of animal welfare—also a set of human derived standards governing how we care for animals under our control. Animal welfare concerns are reflected in laws prohibiting cruelty and criminalizing certain abusive behavior. The debate as illustrated in the New Jersey litigation involves conflicting perspectives on what duties (or rights) we owe animals and on who should decide, using what standards. The contours of the debate have evolved, as reflected in the emergence of "Animal Law" in American legal education. Modern livestock production has also changed significantly, with an increase in confinement production. With these changes, the fundamental legal issues remain divisive, emotional, and elusive of clear resolution.

Legalizing the Debate

The New Jersey case is unique, perhaps even significant, because it involves a focused legal challenge rather than an intellectual debate or noisy rally about whether to serve meat in the cafeteria. As a legalized issue the case could be—and most likely will be if the lower court decision is a guide—decided on narrow legal grounds of statutory interpretation and judicial deference to agency rulemaking. Even a narrow legal ruling will be welcomed by the winning side, but it will not resolve the underlying debate of animal rights versus animal welfare. The court will unlikely resolve that question—the divide between those who endorse traditional livestock husbandry practices and those who allege many of them are inhumane and cruel. Perhaps it is a resolution impossible to achieve in a courtroom, rule-making procedure, or legislative debate—at least not without significant changes in society's relation to food and without extending human-based legal "rights" to animals raised for our purposes.

When stripped of the gloss of litigation and public relations, the debate isn't just about animal welfare; if it were, the "carefully reviewed" decision by the New Jersey Department of Agriculture would resolve the matter. The real debate, at least for those who view it from the perspective of animal welfare, is more complicated. For example, some of those supporting the New Jersey action, such as Farm Sanctuary, do not believe animals should be eaten or that livestock production—modern or otherwise—should exist. For them the debate is a proxy war pitting animal rights and vegetarianism against the continued production and consumption of meat by society—masked as concern for animal welfare and the rule of law. For others, such as the Center for Food Safety, the question is how to balance animal welfare concerns and the profitability of farms, or how strongly economic arguments should be weighed in debates over particular practices.

Validity of Farm Production Practices

No doubt there are well-meaning opponents of New Jersey's rules who believe the practices under scrutiny are in fact "inhumane." Perhaps such opponents would eat the veal chop if they knew the calf was raised in a pen rather than a crate or would enjoy the hamburger more knowing the steer had been anesthetized before being castrated. More likely, however, the food choices of most consumers would not be altered by this knowledge. Moreover, the New Jersey debate is not just a proxy war, but a phony war, to boot, given the heated rhetoric of how the practices in question are employed only by factory farms. The reality is many of the practices, such as castrating young males, are used by small family farmers as well as "factory farms."

Many production practices, such as dehorning, castration, and debeaking, are done for valid production and management reasons and are familiar to every child who grew up with livestock. Of course, notions of what makes a practice "valid" or justified depend on where in the food chain you are located—as is your view of what is inhumane. From a farmer's perspective, or for the veterinarian community, the practices in question are not considered abusive and are not done to be cruel. But for non-farmers or consumers, practices like these sound painful and are easily portrayed as inhumane. Can you imagine doing them to a pet? Animal abuse and cruelty have well-developed bodies of state law prohibiting mistreatment of farm animals. But the case is not only about law but also about rights. Here the debate becomes more complicated because it cannot be denied that some farm practices cause temporary or transient pain to animals. As a young boy the squeals of pigs having rings clamped in their noses made me want to hide. But were their squeals about being grabbed by a human or the ringing? The fear and squeal would be no different if the pig was being grabbed to administer anesthetic or pinch the ring. But the reality of why Dad ringed their noses was undeniable—to stop them from rooting under the fence into the growing corn, or worse yet for their safety, running on the nearby road.

Ringing pigs is not common on farms today but not because any court ruled it inhumane. Instead, most pigs are confined in buildings, no longer free to root the soil. One promising development in our food system and in livestock production—at least for eaters concerned about food quality and the care farm animals receive—is the growing movement to local food and sustainable farming. Organizing producers to market food labeled to inform eaters how it is raised is critical to providing consumers with the quality of food they desire. For years I have worked with Iowa farmers who supply pork for Niman Ranch. The meat is labeled as sustainably and humanely raised on farms certified to meet the Animal Welfare Institute standards of care. The pigs are raised outdoors and not fed animal byproducts or antibiotics. These farmers are committed to providing their pigs the best care possible. Paul Willis, founder of Niman Ranch Pork Company and prominent sustainable Iowa hog farmer, says "our pigs only have one bad day" rather than a lifetime of confinement. But Paul's pigs still end their lives as pork serving the needs of mankind. And the baby males are castrated without anesthesia, not because Paul is cruel, but because alternatives would add unnecessary cost and stress to their production.

Litigation Cannot Resolve the Debate

Are Paul and his colleagues demon "factory farms," or are they caring producers who should be supported and trusted by consumers? Litigation like the present case in New Jersey diverts citizens and animal activists (at least those really interested in improving conditions for livestock) from supporting farmers committed to taking the best care of their animals. If people oppose factory farms—and there are many legitimate concerns about social ills of industrialized production—there are more direct ways to confront them rather than arguing in court that their practices are inhumane. Pursuing environmental compliance, raising public awareness of health risks from air pollution, and assuring worker safety are all more direct avenues—as are market-based actions of not buying their products. Recent actions by major food retailers, such as McDonald's decision to require egg suppliers to increase the spacing given hens and dairies refusing to purchase milk produced with rBST (recombinant bovine somatotropin) or artificial growth hormones, show how sensitive the market can be to consumer concerns. Animal welfare issues are part of the marketer-consumer context.

My arguments may be suspect for opponents of New Jersey's livestock rules. As a farm boy, meat eater, former cattle owner, and agricultural law professor—whatever that is—am I tainted by complicity in a lifestyle of cruelty and animal neglect? Maybe so, but doubters should also know I founded the local Slow Food convivium in Des Moines to help eaters experience the joys of food, sell produce to restaurants from our market garden, own many pets, freely criticize industrial agriculture, and advise small livestock producers seeking markets to support their practices. Rather than reduce the debate to narrow legal definitions like "inhumane" that are freighted with our own ideas of morality and ethics, it might be more effective to put the debate about livestock care into a larger context of social relations.

Consider two examples that question whether our perceptions of cruel and inhumane are more imagined than real. First is circumcising baby boys—done for health or religious reasons—something I experienced 54 years ago. I do not remember the event, but no doubt I cried, bled, and felt some pain. I cannot say I would like to do it again today, but does that make my parent's decision cruel or inhumane? Should we outlaw the practice or require it be done under anesthesia—and if so local or general? Which treatment would threaten a baby's health more? Who should decide? The second illustration is for law students. Remember the first day of class with a professor that used the Socratic method [a method where questions are used to arrive at conclusions or argue a point]? Some may have thrived, but if you were like me you were terrified—at least at first. But you got used to it, you survived, and if the reasoning behind Socratic method can be trusted, it made you a better student and lawyer. Was it inhumane or cruel? Is it a legitimate teaching method—herd health management so to speak—or should it be outlawed or challenged as illegal under Michigan's anti-hazing law? Whose standards should prevail—professors' or student-rights activists'?

When I started attending the Association of American Law Schools (AALS) meetings we created an Agricultural Law section. In the mid 1980's when the farm financial crisis threatened the lives and livelihoods of thousands of farm families, the section was lucky to attract ten colleagues to discuss helping farmers save their farms. At the same time the Animal Law section emerged and the size of their sessions grew. Agricultural law still struggles to attract twenty colleagues to sessions. At the 2008 New York meeting, our themes were the environment and alternative energy and in 2007, farmer-worker issues. Animal law has had far healthier growth and today is taught at many schools. In academia the rights of animals are apparently more attractive than those of farmers, eaters, or workers. The New York session "Debating Animals as Legal Persons" was packed. But a statement in the program description puzzled me—"No quintessentially 'human' characteristic definitively sets humans apart from other animals." This seed sprouts the New Jersey litigation and our debate.

Think about it for a moment. Do you agree: have you ever been confused you were something other than a human or have you mistaken an animal as a human (regardless of how your dog might answer)? Of course not—there is a human essence that defines us all. But is the statement true, legally, or can we make it true? This incident is paralleled by another New Jersey story—the tragic tale of the landscaper, a human you might note, severely mauled by an employer's dog. Under New Jersey law he recovered damages for the injuries but the dog was impounded and sentenced to die as a vicious animal. What has since unfolded illustrates our mixed, perhaps even misguided, attitudes about animal rights. The November 20,

2007, *New York Times* headline says it all, "A Landscaper is Mauled, and an Outpouring of Sympathy Goes to the Dog." Yes, we are animals too and in a legal democracy we can choose who we like more. But do we need to deny our humanity to promote animal rights? Perhaps those who rally for the dog are just saying landscapers and humans deserve our one bad day too. Animal welfare or animal rights—good luck bridging the divide.

CHAPTER 4

National Defense
Has Priority over the
Welfare of Animals

Case Overview

Winter, Secretary of the Navy v. Natural Resources Defense Council (2008)

Sonar is a technology that uses sound waves to locate objects underwater. It was first used by the U.S. Navy to detect submarines during World War II. Later, with the advent of nuclear and modern diesel-electric submarines, the original low frequency active sonar (LFAS) proved inadequate for some purposes and more powerful mid-frequency active (MFA) sonar systems were developed. Antisubmarine warfare depends heavily on sonar; without it, there would be no way to evade or attack enemy subs. Yet it is a highly complex technology that requires well-trained, experienced operators.

It is now known that utilization of underwater sound waves is not limited to humans, as was once assumed. In the late twentieth century it was discovered that marine mammals such as whales and dolphins depend on them, too. The purposes for which they use them are not thoroughly understood, but scientists believe that the sonar produced by submarines can interfere with the sea mammals' basic biological functions, such as foraging and mating. Furthermore, in the mid-1990s a link was found between the use of military sonar and mass strandings of whales on beaches or in shallow water. Examination of stranded whales revealed bleeding from their ears and eyes caused by excessive sound, which damaged their hearing and could have confused them.

Naturally, animal welfare activists are opposed to harming whales and dolphins. Though most of them concede that sonar is necessary in combat situations, they object to its use merely for training. Training of sonar operators is essential to national defense, however, because without it, sonar could not be used effectively in combat if such a situation ever arose.

This would result in the deaths of not only submarine crews but also the people the subs are intended to protect. The navy is required by law to do everything it can to minimize the potential harm to marine mammals, but it cannot eliminate sonar training exercises.

This conflict has resulted in many lawsuits. In 2006 a suit against the navy was filed by the Natural Resources Defense Council (NRDC) on the basis of MFA sonar exercises conducted in violation of the National Environmental Policy Act (NEPA), the Marine Mammal Protection Act (MMPA), and the Endangered Species Act (ESA). The court banned the use of submarine-hunting sonar in training missions off Southern California pending adoption of safeguards for marine mammals, and a settlement involving mitigation measures was reached. The next year, the NRDC filed a new suit objecting to specific exercises that the navy was planning. The court again issued a temporary restraining order, which the court of appeals at first stayed, but later that court reversed itself and allowed a new restraining order (injunction) to be issued, whereupon the navy sought help from President George W. Bush. The president granted the navy an exemption because he considered the exercises crucial to national security. A federal judge, however, ruled that despite President Bush's decision, the navy must follow environmental laws and obey the court injunction, and the court of appeals upheld this ruling. The navy then appealed to the U.S. Supreme Court.

The Supreme Court did not decide the issue of whether the navy is required to obey all environmental laws; it merely ruled that the restraining order against the exercises was not warranted. In its opinion (which was signed by only five of the nine justices) it made clear that the majority considered maintaining a military defense capability more important than protecting marine life. This has upset many environmentalists, while many people concerned about national security have been troubled by the narrowness of the decision and fear future cases where environmental concerns may trump national security.

Majority Opinion: The Need to Conduct Naval Training Exercises Outweighs Protection of Marine Mammals

John Roberts

John Roberts became the chief justice of the United States in 2005. He is a conservative judge who believes in interpreting the Constitution strictly. The following is his written opinion for the majority in Winter v. Natural Resources Defense Council, *which involved a dispute between the U.S. Navy and an environmental organization that objected to the use of sonar on grounds that it could harm marine mammals. He first explains the reasons why sonar is essential to naval training exercises, then the arguments about harm to whales and dolphins presented by the Natural Resources Defense Council. The actual question before the Court, he points out, is not whether sonar should ever be used in training, but whether the lower court was justified in issuing an injunction preventing its unrestricted use before the navy had submitted an environmental impact statement. The Court decided that since the training was essential to*

John Roberts, majority opinion, *Winter, Secretary of the Navy, et al. v. Natural Resources Defense Council*, U.S. Supreme Court, October 8, 2008.

national security, there was insufficient basis for the injunction and that the lower court abused its discretion by imposing the the restrictions.

"To be prepared for war is one of the most effectual means of preserving peace." So said George Washington in his first Annual Address to Congress, 218 years ago. One of the most important ways the Navy prepares for war is through integrated training exercises at sea. These exercises include training in the use of modern sonar to detect and track enemy submarines, something the Navy has done for the past 40 years. The plaintiffs complained that the Navy's sonar training program harmed marine mammals, and that the Navy should have prepared an environmental impact statement before commencing its latest round of training exercises. The Court of Appeals upheld a preliminary injunction imposing restrictions on the Navy's sonar training, even though that court acknowledged that "the record contains no evidence that marine mammals have been harmed" by the Navy's exercises.

The Court of Appeals was wrong, and its decision is reversed.

The Naval Training Exercises

The Navy deploys its forces in "strike groups," which are groups of surface ships, submarines, and aircraft centered around either an aircraft carrier or an amphibious assault ship. Seamless coordination among strike-group assets is critical. Before deploying a strike group, the Navy requires extensive integrated training in analysis and prioritization of threats, execution of military missions, and maintenance of force protection.

Antisubmarine warfare is currently the Pacific Fleet's top war-fighting priority. Modern diesel-electric submarines pose a significant threat to Navy vessels because they can operate almost silently, making them extremely difficult to detect and track. Potential adversaries of the United States possess at least 300 of these submarines.

The most effective technology for identifying submerged diesel-electric submarines within their torpedo range is active sonar, which involves emitting pulses of sound underwater and then receiving the acoustic waves that echo off the target. Active sonar is a particularly useful tool because it provides both the bearing and the distance of target submarines; it is also sensitive enough to allow the Navy to track enemy submarines that are quieter than the surrounding marine environment. This case concerns the Navy's use of "mid-frequency active" (MFA) sonar, which transmits sound waves at frequencies between 1 kHz [kiloHertz, or one thousand cycles per second] and 10 kHz.

Not surprisingly, MFA sonar is a complex technology, and sonar operators must undergo extensive training to become proficient in its use. Sonar reception can be affected by countless different factors, including the time of day, water density, salinity, currents, weather conditions, and the contours of the sea floor. When working as part of a strike group, sonar operators must be able to coordinate with other Navy ships and planes while avoiding interference. The Navy conducts regular training exercises under realistic conditions to ensure that sonar operators are thoroughly skilled in its use in a variety of situations.

The waters off the coast of southern California (SOCAL) are an ideal location for conducting integrated training exercises, as this is the only area on the west coast that is relatively close to land, air, and sea bases, as well as amphibious landing areas. . . . The use of MFA sonar during these exercises is "mission-critical," given that MFA sonar is the only proven method of identifying submerged diesel-electric submarines operating on battery power.

Sharing the waters in the SOCAL operating area are at least 37 species of marine mammals, including dolphins, whales, and sea lions. The parties strongly dispute the extent to which the Navy's training activities will harm those animals or disrupt their behavioral patterns. The Navy emphasizes that it has used MFA sonar during training exercises in SOCAL for 40 years, without a single documented sonar-related injury to any marine mammal. The Navy asserts that, at most, MFA sonar may cause temporary hearing loss or brief disruptions of marine mammals' behavioral patterns.

The Threat to Marine Mammals

The plaintiffs are the Natural Resources Defense Council, Jean-Michel Cousteau (an environmental enthusiast and filmmaker), and several other groups devoted to the protection of marine mammals and ocean habitats. They contend that MFA sonar can cause much more serious injuries to marine mammals than the Navy acknowledges, including permanent hearing loss, decompression sickness, and major behavioral disruptions. According to the plaintiffs, several mass strandings of marine mammals (outside of SOCAL) have been "associated" with the use of active sonar. They argue that certain species of marine mammals—such as beaked whales—are uniquely susceptible to injury from active sonar; these injuries would not necessarily be detected by the Navy, given that beaked whales are "very deep divers" that spend little time at the surface. . . .

The National Environmental Policy Act of 1969 (NEPA), requires federal agencies "to the fullest extent possible" to prepare an environmental impact statement (EIS) for "every . . . major Federal actio[n] significantly affecting the quality of the human environment." An agency is not required to prepare a full EIS if it determines—based on a shorter environmental assessment (EA)—that the proposed action will not have a significant impact on the environment.

In February 2007, the Navy issued an EA concluding that the 14 SOCAL training exercises scheduled through January 2009 would not have a significant impact on the environment. . . .

The Navy's computer models predicted that the SOCAL training exercises would cause only eight Level A harassments of common dolphins each year, and that even these injuries could be avoided through the Navy's voluntary mitigation measures, given that dolphins travel in large pods easily located by Navy lookouts. . . .

Lower Court Actions

In light of its conclusion that the SOCAL training exercises would not have a significant impact on the environment, the Navy determined that it was unnecessary to prepare a full EIS.

Shortly after the Navy released its EA, the plaintiffs sued the Navy, seeking declaratory and injunctive relief on the grounds that the Navy's SOCAL training exercises violated NEPA, the Endangered Species Act of 1973 (ESA), and the Coastal Zone Management Act of 1972 (CZMA). The District Court granted plaintiffs' motion for a preliminary injunction and prohibited the Navy from using MFA sonar during its remaining training exercises. . . .

The Navy filed an emergency appeal, and the Ninth Circuit stayed the injunction pending appeal. After hearing oral argument, the Court of Appeals agreed with the District Court that preliminary injunctive relief was appropriate. The appellate court concluded, however, that a blanket injunction prohibiting the Navy from using MFA sonar in SOCAL was overbroad. . . .

On remand, the District Court entered a new preliminary injunction allowing the Navy to use MFA sonar only as long as it implemented the following mitigation measures (in addition to the measures the Navy had adopted pursuant to its MMPA [Marine Mammal Protection Act] exemption): (1) imposing a 12-mile "exclusion zone" from the coastline; (2) using lookouts to conduct additional monitoring for marine mammals; (3) restricting the use of "helicopter-dipping" sonar; (4) limiting the use of MFA sonar in geographic "choke points"; (5) shutting down MFA sonar when a marine mammal is spotted within 2,200 yards of a vessel; and (6) powering down MFA sonar by 6 dB [decibels] during significant surface ducting conditions, in which sound travels further than it otherwise would due to temperature differences in adjacent layers of water. The Navy filed a notice of appeal, challenging only the last two restrictions.

The Navy then sought relief from the Executive Branch. The President [George W. Bush] granted the Navy an exemption from the CZMA. . . . The President determined that continuation of the exercises as limited by the Navy was "essential to national security." He concluded that compliance with the District Court's injunction would "undermine the Navy's ability to conduct realistic training exercises that are necessary to ensure the combat effectiveness of . . . strike groups."

Simultaneously, the Council on Environmental Quality (CEQ) authorized the Navy to implement "alternative arrangements" to NEPA compliance in light of "emergency circumstances." . . .

In light of these actions, the Navy then moved to vacate the District Court's injunction with respect to the 2,200-yard shutdown zone and the restrictions on training in surface ducting conditions. The District Court refused to do so, and the Court of Appeals affirmed. The Ninth Circuit held that there was a serious question regarding whether the CEQ's interpretation of the "emergency circumstances" regulation was lawful. Specifically, the court questioned whether there was a true "emergency" in this case, given that the Navy has been on notice of its obligation to comply with NEPA from the moment it first planned the SOCAL training exercises. . . .

The Court of Appeals further determined that plaintiffs had carried their burden of establishing a "possibility" of irreparable injury. Even under the Navy's own figures, the court concluded, the training exercises would cause 564 physical injuries to marine mammals, as well as 170,000 disturbances of marine mammals' behavior. Lastly, the Court of Appeals held that the balance of hardships and consideration of the public interest weighed in favor of the plaintiffs. . . .

Basis for a Preliminary Injunction

A plaintiff seeking a preliminary injunction must establish that he is likely to succeed on the merits, that he is likely to suffer irreparable harm in the absence of preliminary relief, that the balance of equities tips in his favor, and that an injunction is in the public interest.

The District Court and the Ninth Circuit concluded that plaintiffs have shown a likelihood of success on the merits of their NEPA claim. The Navy strongly disputes this determination. . . .

The District Court and the Ninth Circuit also held that when a plaintiff demonstrates a strong likelihood of prevailing on the merits, a preliminary injunction may be entered based only on a "possibility" of irreparable harm. The lower courts held that plaintiffs had met this standard because the scientific studies, declarations, and other evidence in the record established to "a near certainty" that the Navy's training exercises would cause irreparable harm to the environment.

The Navy challenges these holdings, arguing that plaintiffs must demonstrate a likelihood of irreparable injury—not just a possibility—in order to obtain preliminary relief. . . . And even if MFA sonar does cause a limited number of injuries to individual *marine mammals*, the Navy asserts that plaintiffs have failed to offer evidence of species-level harm that would adversely affect *their* scientific, recreational, and ecological interests. . . .

We agree with the Navy that the Ninth Circuit's "possibility" standard is too lenient. Our frequently reiterated standard requires plaintiffs seeking preliminary relief to demonstrate that irreparable injury is *likely* in the absence of an injunction. . . .

The District Court originally found irreparable harm from sonar-training, exercises generally. But by the time of the District Court's final decision, the Navy challenged only two of six restrictions imposed by the court. The District Court did not reconsider the likelihood of irreparable harm in light of the four restrictions not challenged by the Navy. This failure is significant in light of the District Court's own statement that the 12-mile exclusion zone from the coastline—one of the unchallenged mitigation restrictions—"would bar the use of MFA sonar in a significant portion of important marine mammal habitat."

We also find it pertinent that this is not a case in which the defendant is conducting a new type of activity with completely unknown effects on the environment. . . . Part of the harm NEPA attempts to prevent in requiring an EIS is that, without one, there may be little if any information about prospective environmental harms and potential mitigating measures. Here, in contrast, the plaintiffs are seeking to enjoin—or substantially restrict—training exercises that have been taking place in SOCAL for the last 40 years. . . .

Even if plaintiffs have shown irreparable injury from the Navy's training exercises, any such injury is outweighed by the public interest and the Navy's interest in effective, realistic training of its sailors. . . .

Impact of the Injunction on the Navy

A preliminary injunction is an extraordinary remedy never awarded as of right. In each case, courts "must balance the competing claims of injury and must consider the effect on each party of the granting or withholding of the requested relief." (*Amoco Production Co.* [*v. Gambell*]) . . . In this case, the District Court and the Ninth Circuit significantly understated the burden the preliminary injunction would impose on the Navy's ability to conduct realistic training exercises, and the injunction's consequent adverse impact on the public interest in national defense.

This case involves "complex, subtle, and professional decisions as to the composition, training, equipping, and control of a military force," which are "essentially professional military judgments." (*Gilligan v. Morgan.*) We "give great deference to the professional judgment of military authorities concerning the relative importance of a particular interest." (*Goldman v. Weinberger*) . . .

Here, the record contains declarations from some of the Navy's most senior officers, all of whom underscored the threat posed by enemy submarines and the need for extensive sonar training to counter this threat. . . .

These interests must be weighed against the possible harm to the ecological, scientific, and recreational interests that are legitimately before this Court. Plaintiffs have submitted declarations asserting that they take whale watching trips, observe marine mammals underwater, conduct scientific research on marine mammals, and photograph these animals in their natural habitats. Plaintiffs contend that the Navy's use of MFA sonar will injure marine mammals or alter their behavioral patterns, impairing plaintiffs' ability to study and observe the animals.

While we do not question the seriousness of these interests, we conclude that the balance of equities and consideration of the overall public interest in this case tip strongly in favor of the Navy. For the plaintiffs, the most serious possible injury would be harm to an unknown number of the marine mammals that they study and observe. In contrast, forcing the Navy to deploy an inadequately trained antisubmarine force jeopardizes the safety of the fleet. Active sonar is the only reliable technology for detecting and tracking enemy diesel-electric submarines, and the President—the Commander in Chief—has determined that training with active sonar is "essential to national security."

The public interest in conducting training exercises with active sonar under realistic conditions plainly outweighs the interests advanced by the plaintiffs. Of course, military interests do not always trump other considerations, and we have not held that they do. In this case, however, the proper determination of where the public interest lies does not strike us as a close question. . . .

The Court of Appeals held that the balance of equities and the public interest favored the plaintiffs, largely based on its view that the preliminary injunction would not in fact impose a significant burden on the Navy's ability to conduct its training exercises and certify its strike groups. . . .

The preliminary injunction requires the Navy to shut down its MFA sonar if a marine mammal is detected within 2,200 yards of a sonar-emitting vessel. The Ninth Circuit stated that the 2,200-yard shutdown zone would not be overly burdensome because sightings of marine mammals during training exercises are relatively rare. But regardless of the frequency of marine mammal sightings, the injunction will greatly increase the size of the shutdown zone. Pursuant to its exemption from the MMPA, the Navy agreed to reduce the power of its MFA sonar at 1,000 yards and 500 yards, and to completely turn off the system at 200 yards. The District Court's injunction does not include a graduated power-down, instead requiring a total shutdown of MFA sonar if a marine mammal is detected within 2,200 yards of a sonar-emitting vessel. There is an exponential relationship between radius length and surface area (Area $= \pi\, r^2$). Increasing the radius of the shutdown zone from 200 to 2,200 yards would accordingly expand the surface area of the shutdown zone by a factor of over 100.

The lower courts did not give sufficient weight to the views of several top Navy officers, who emphasized that because training scenarios can take several days to develop, each additional shutdown can result in the loss of several days' worth of training. . . . Even if there is a low likelihood of a marine mammal sighting, the preliminary injunction would clearly increase the number of disruptive sonar shutdowns the Navy is forced to perform during its SOCAL training exercises.

The Court of Appeals also concluded that the 2,200-yard shutdown zone would not be overly burdensome because the Navy had shut down MFA sonar 27 times during its eight prior training exercises in SOCAL; in several of these cases, the Navy turned off its sonar when marine mammals were spotted well beyond the Navy's self-imposed 200-yard shutdown zone. . . . The record supports the Navy's contention that its shutdowns of MFA sonar during prior training exercises only occurred during tactically insignificant times; those voluntary shutdowns do not justify the District Court's imposition of a mandatory 2,200-yard shutdown zone.

Lastly, the Ninth Circuit stated that a 2,200-yard shutdown zone was feasible because the Navy had previously adopted a 2,000-meter zone for low-frequency active (LFA) sonar. The Court of Appeals failed to give sufficient weight to the fact that LFA sonar is used for long-range detection of enemy submarines, and thus its use and shutdown involve tactical considerations quite different from those associated with MFA sonar. . . .

The Ninth Circuit determined that the power-down requirement during surface ducting conditions was unlikely to affect certification of the Navy's strike groups because surface ducting occurs relatively rarely, and the Navy has previously certified strike groups that did not train under such conditions. This reasoning is backwards. Given that surface ducting is both rare and unpredictable, it is especially important for the Navy to be able to train under these conditions when they occur. . . .

The Injunction Was Unjustified

The District Court acknowledged that "'the imposition of these mitigation measures will require the Navy to alter and adapt the way it conducts antisubmarine warfare training—a substantial challenge. Nevertheless, evidence presented to the Court reflects that the Navy has employed mitigation measures in the past, without sacrificing training objectives.'" Apparently no good deed goes unpunished. The fact that the Navy has taken measures in the past to address concerns about marine mammals—or, for that matter, has elected not to challenge four additional restrictions imposed by the District Court in this case, hardly means that other, more intrusive restrictions pose no threat to preparedness for war.

The Court of Appeals concluded its opinion by stating that "the Navy may return to the district court to request relief on an emergency basis" if the preliminary injunction "actually result[s] in an inability to train and certify sufficient naval forces to provide for the national defense." This is cold comfort to the Navy. The Navy contends that the injunction will hinder efforts to train sonar operators under realistic conditions, ultimately leaving strike groups more vulnerable to enemy submarines. Unlike the Ninth Circuit, we do not think the Navy is required to wait until the injunction "actually result[s] in an inability to train . . . sufficient naval forces for the national defense" before seeking its dissolution. By then it may be too late. . . .

The factors examined above—the balance of equities and consideration of the public interest—are pertinent in assessing the propriety of any injunctive relief, preliminary or permanent. Given that the ultimate legal claim is that the Navy must prepare an EIS, not that it must cease sonar training, there is no basis for enjoining such training in a manner credibly alleged to pose a serious threat to national security. This is particularly true in light of the fact that the training has been going on for 40 years with no documented episode of harm to a marine mammal. A court concluding that the Navy is required to prepare an EIS has many remedial tools at its disposal, including declaratory relief or an injunction tailored to the preparation of an EIS rather than the Navy's training in the interim. In the meantime, we see no basis for jeopardizing national security, as the present injunction does. . . .

President Theodore Roosevelt explained that "the only way in which a navy can ever be made efficient is by practice at sea, under all the conditions which would have to be met if war existed." We do not discount the importance of plaintiffs' ecological, scientific, and recreational interests in marine mammals. Those interests, however, are plainly outweighed by the Navy's need to conduct realistic training exercises to ensure that it is able to neutralize the threat posed by enemy submarines. The District Court abused its discretion by imposing a 2,200-yard shutdown zone and by requiring the Navy to power down its MFA sonar during significant surface ducting conditions. The judgment of the Court of Appeals is reversed, and the preliminary injunction is vacated to the extent it has been challenged by the Navy.

> "This likely harm [to marine mammals] . . . cannot be lightly dismissed, even in the face of an alleged risk to the effectiveness of the Navy's 14 training exercises."

Dissenting Opinion: Defense Considerations Do Not Authorize the Navy to Violate the Law

Ruth Bader Ginsburg

Ruth Bader Ginsburg has been a justice of the Supreme Court since 1993 and is one of its most liberal members. The following is her dissenting opinion in Winter v. Natural Resources Defense Council, *in which she argues that the U.S. Navy should have prepared an environmental impact statement (EIS) before conducting training exercises using sonar, instead of planning to do so afterwards. By going ahead without one, she says, it thwarted the purpose of an EIS. The navy's own assessment predicted considerable harm to marine mammals from the sonar, and she believes the likelihood of such harm justified the restrictions on the exercises imposed by the lower court. If the navy objected, she argues, it should have sought an exemption from the law from Congress rather than from the president. In her opinion, the national defense interests served by the training did not authorize it to violate a statutory command.*

Ruth Bader Ginsburg, dissenting opinion, *Winter, Secretary of the Navy, et al. v. Natural Resources Defense Council,* U.S. Supreme Court, October 8, 2008.

The central question in this action under the National Environmental Policy Act of 1969 (NEPA) was whether the Navy must prepare an environmental impact statement (EIS). The Navy does not challenge its obligation to do so, and it represents that the EIS will be complete in January 2009—one month after the instant exercises [that is, the exercises under consideration by the Court at that time] conclude. If the Navy had completed the EIS before taking action, as NEPA instructs, the parties and the public could have benefited from the environmental analysis—and the Navy's training could have proceeded without interruption. Instead, the Navy acted first, and thus thwarted the very purpose an EIS is intended to serve. To justify its course, the Navy sought dispensation not from Congress, but from an executive council that lacks authority to countermand or revise NEPA's requirements. I would hold that, in imposing manageable measures to mitigate harm until completion of the EIS, the District Court conscientiously balanced the equities and did not abuse its discretion.

The Navy Delayed Its EIS

In December 2006, the Navy announced its intent to prepare an EIS to address the potential environmental effects of its naval readiness activities in the Southern California (SOCAL) Range Complex. These readiness activities include expansion and intensification of naval training, as well as research, development, and testing of various systems and weapons.

In February 2007, seeking to commence training before completion of the EIS, the Navy prepared an Environmental Assessment (EA) for the 14 exercises it planned to undertake in the interim. On February 12, the Navy concluded the EA with a finding of no significant impact. The same day, the Navy commenced its training exercises.

On March 22, 2007, the Natural Resources Defense Council (NRDC) filed suit in the U. S. District Court for the Central District of California, seeking declaratory and injunctive relief based on the Navy's alleged violations of NEPA and other environmental statutes. As relevant here, the District Court determined that NRDC was likely to succeed on its NEPA claim and that equitable principles warranted preliminary relief. On August 7, 2007, the court enjoined the Navy's use of mid-frequency active (MFA) sonar during the 11 remaining exercises at issue.

On August 31, the Court of Appeals for the Ninth Circuit stayed the injunction pending disposition of the Navy's appeal, and the Navy proceeded with two more exercises. In a November 13 order, the Court of Appeals vacated the stay, stating that NRDC had shown "a strong likelihood of success on the merits" and that preliminary injunctive relief was appropriate. The Court of Appeals remanded, however, instructing the District Court to provide mitigation measures under which the Navy could conduct its remaining exercises. . . .

On January 3, 2008, the District Court entered a modified preliminary injunction imposing six mitigation measures. The court revised the modified injunction slightly on January 10 in response to filings by the Navy, and four days later, denied the Navy's application for a stay pending appeal.

On the following day, January 15, the Council on Environmental Quality (CEQ), an advisory body within the Executive Office of the President, responded to the Navy's request for "alternative arrangements" for NEPA compliance. The "arrangements" CEQ set out purported to permit the Navy to continue its training without timely environmental review. The Navy accepted the arrangements on the same day.

The Navy then filed an emergency motion in the Court of Appeals requesting immediate vacatur [voiding] of the District Court's modified injunction. CEQ's action, the Navy urged, eliminated the injunction's legal foundation. In the alternative, the Navy sought a stay of two aspects of the injunction pending its appeal: the 2,200-yard mandatory shutdown zone and the power-down requirement in significant surface ducting conditions. While targeting in its stay application only two of the six measures imposed by the District Court, the Navy explicitly reserved the right to challenge on appeal each of the six mitigation measures. Responding to the Navy's emergency motion, the Court of Appeals remanded the matter to allow the District Court to determine in the first instance the effect of the intervening executive action. Pending its own consideration of the Navy's motion, the District Court stayed the injunction, and the Navy conducted its sixth exercise.

On February 4, after briefing and oral argument, the District Court denied the Navy's motion. The Navy appealed, reiterating its position that CEQ's action eliminated all justification for the injunction. The Navy also argued that vacatur of the entire injunction was required irrespective of CEQ's action, in part because the "conditions imposed, in particular the 2,200 yard mandatory shutdown zone and the six decibel (75%) power-down in significant surface ducting conditions, severely degrade the Navy's training." In the February 29 decision now under review, the Court of Appeals affirmed the District Court's judgment. The Navy has continued training in the meantime and plans to complete its final exercise in December 2008.

As the procedural history indicates, the courts below determined that an EIS was required for the 14 exercises. The Navy does not challenge that decision in this Court. Instead, the Navy defends its failure to complete an EIS before launching the exercises based upon CEQ's "alternative arrangements"—arrangements the Navy sought and obtained in order to overcome the lower courts' rulings. As explained below, the Navy's actions undermined NEPA and took an extraordinary course.

An EIS Is Important

NEPA "promotes its sweeping commitment" to environmental integrity "by focusing Government and public attention on the environmental effects of proposed agency action." (*Marsh v. Oregon Natural Resources Council*). "By so focusing agency attention, NEPA ensures that the agency will not act on incomplete information, only to regret its decision after it is too late to correct."

The EIS is NEPA's core requirement. . . . The EIS requirement "ensures that important effects will not be overlooked or underestimated only to be discovered after resources have been committed or the die otherwise cast."

"Publication of an EIS . . . also serves a larger informational role." It demonstrates that an agency has indeed considered environmental concerns, and "perhaps more significantly, provides a springboard for public comment." At the same time, it affords other affected governmental bodies "notice of the expected consequences and the opportunity to plan and implement corrective measures in a timely manner."

In light of these objectives, the timing of an EIS is critical. . . .

The Navy's publication of its EIS in this case, scheduled to occur *after* the 14 exercises are completed, defeats NEPA's informational and participatory purposes. The Navy's inverted timing, it bears emphasis, is the very reason why the District Court had to confront the question of mitigation measures at all. Had the Navy prepared a legally sufficient EIS before beginning the SOCAL exercises, NEPA would have functioned as its drafters intended: The EIS process and associated public input might have convinced the Navy voluntarily to adopt mitigation measures, but NEPA itself would not have impeded the Navy's exercises.

The Navy had other options. Most importantly, it could have requested assistance from Congress. The Government has sometimes obtained congressional authorization to proceed with planned activities without fulfilling NEPA's requirements.

Rather than resorting to Congress, the Navy "sought relief from the Executive Branch." On January 10, 2008, the Navy asked CEQ, adviser to the President, to approve alternative arrangements for NEPA compliance. The next day, the Navy submitted supplementary material to CEQ, including the Navy's EA and after-action reports, the District Court's orders, and two analyses by the National Marine Fisheries Service (NMFS). Neither the Navy nor CEQ notified NRDC, and CEQ did not request or consider any of the materials underlying the District Court orders it addressed.

Four days later, on January 15, the Chairman of CEQ issued a letter to the Secretary of the Navy. Repeating the Navy's submissions with little independent analysis, the letter stated that the District Court's orders posed risks to the Navy's training exercises. . . .

The alternative arrangements CEQ set forth do not vindicate NEPA's objectives. The arrangements provide for "public participation measures," which require the Navy to provide notices of the alternative arrangements. The notices must "seek input on the process for reviewing post-exercise assessments" and "include an offer to meet jointly with Navy representatives . . . and CEQ to discuss the alternative arrangements." The alternative arrangements also describe the Navy's existing research and mitigation efforts.

CEQ's hasty decision on a one-sided record is no substitute for the District Court's considered judgment based on a two-sided record. More fundamentally, even an exemplary CEQ review could not have effected the short circuit the Navy sought. CEQ lacks authority to absolve an agency of its statutory duty to prepare an EIS. NEPA established CEQ to assist and advise the President on environmental policy, and a 1977 Executive Order charged CEQ with issuing regulations to federal agencies for implementation of NEPA's procedural provisions. This Court has recognized that CEQ's regulations are entitled to "substantial deference," and CEQ may play an important consultative role in emergency circumstances, but we have never suggested that CEQ could eliminate the statute's command. If the Navy sought to avoid its NEPA obligations, its remedy lay in the Legislative Branch. The Navy's alternative course—rapid, self-serving resort to an office in the White House—is surely not what Congress had in mind when it instructed agencies to comply with NEPA "to the fullest extent possible."

Harm Was Likely

Flexibility is a hallmark of equity jurisdiction. . . . Consistent with equity's character, courts do not insist that litigants uniformly show a particular, predetermined quantum of probable success or injury before awarding equitable relief. Instead, courts have evaluated claims for equitable relief on a "sliding scale," sometimes awarding relief based on a lower likelihood of harm when the likelihood of success is very high. This Court has never rejected that formulation, and I do not believe it does so today.

Equity's flexibility is important in the NEPA context. Because an EIS is the tool for *uncovering* environmental harm, environmental plaintiffs may often rely more heavily on their probability of success than the likelihood of harm. The Court is correct that relief is not warranted "simply to prevent the possibility of some remote future injury." "However, the injury need not have been inflicted when application is made or be certain to occur; a strong threat of irreparable injury before trial is an adequate basis." I agree with the District Court that NRDC made the required showing here.

The Navy's own EA predicted substantial and irreparable harm to marine mammals. Sonar is linked to mass strandings of marine mammals, hemorrhaging around the brain and ears, acute spongiotic changes in the central nervous system, and lesions in vital organs. As the Ninth Circuit noted, the EA predicts that the Navy's "use of MFA sonar in the SOCAL exercises will result in 564 instances of physical injury including permanent hearing loss (Level A harassment) and nearly 170,000 behavioral disturbances (Level B harassment), more than 8,000 of which would also involve temporary hearing loss." . . .

The majority acknowledges the lower courts' findings, but also states that the EA predicted "only eight Level A harassments of common dolphins each year" and "274 Level B harassments of beaked whales per year, none of which would result in permanent injury." Those numbers do not fully capture the EA's predictions.

The EA classified the harassments of beaked whales as Level A, not Level B. The EA does indeed state that "modeling predicts non-injurious Level B exposures." But, as the majority correctly notes, the EA also states that "all beaked whale exposures are counted as Level A." The EA counted the predicted exposures as Level A "[b]y Navy policy developed in conjunction with NMFS." The record reflects "the known sensitivity of these species to tactical sonar," and as the majority acknowledges, beaked whales are difficult to study. Further, as the Ninth Circuit noted, "the EA . . . maintained that the methodology used was based on the 'best available science.'"

In my view, this likely harm—170,000 behavioral disturbances, including 8,000 instances of temporary hearing loss; and 564 Level A harms, including 436 injuries to a beaked whale population numbering only 1,121—cannot be lightly dismissed, even in the face of an alleged risk to the effectiveness of the Navy's 14 training exercises. There is no doubt that the training exercises serve critical interests. But those interests do not authorize the Navy to violate a statutory command, especially when recourse to the Legislature remains open. . . .

In light of the likely, substantial harm to the environment, NRDC's almost inevitable success on the merits of its claim that NEPA required the Navy to prepare an EIS, the history of this litigation, and the public interest, I cannot agree that the mitigation measures the District Court imposed signal an abuse of discretion.

For the reasons stated, I would affirm the judgment of the Ninth Circuit.

"The justices had a lot of tough questions for both sides, which is what you would expect in a Supreme Court case. If it were an easy call, why would it wind up in the highest court in the land?"

The Court Seemed Closely Divided in *Winter v. NRDC*

Scott Dodd

Scott Dodd is the editorial manager for the Natural Resources Defense Council's Web site. In the following report from its blog Switchboard, *which he wrote on the day the Supreme Court heard arguments in* Winter v. Natural Resources Defense Council, *he describes the questions asked by the justices. The attorneys for both sides faced tough scrutiny, he says, and were interrupted with questions many times during their presentations. The attorney for the navy disputed the claim that a large number of marine mammals would be harmed by its sonar training exercises, while the NRDC attorney argued that many whale strandings have been caused by sonar. Some of the justices appeared to be supporting one, some the other, but reporters experienced with the Supreme Court believed that they were closely divided.*

Lawyers from NRDC [the Natural Resources Defense Council] and the U.S. Navy faced tough scrutiny on everything from beaked whale strandings to the separation of powers as they argued before the U.S. Supreme Court.

Scott Dodd, "Switchboard: Updated Report from the Court: NRDC and the Navy Face Off over Sonar's Harm to Whales," NRDC.org, October 8, 2008. Reproduced with permission from the Natural Resources Defense Council.

In a case that could determine whether the Navy is doing enough to protect marine mammals from intense blasts of sonar, the justices peppered the parties with questions on a number of legal and factual fronts.

One of the most entertaining exchanges came when Justice Stephen Breyer asked why the military should be relied on to conduct environmental impact studies—one of the key requirements that NRDC argues was needed in this case. "The whole point of the armed forces is to hurt the environment," Breyer said, prompting laughter from the audience of about 250 in the courtroom.

Richard Kendall, who argued on behalf of NRDC, countered that "the whole point of the armed forces is to do the least amount of harm possible to the environment."

"When they go on a bombing mission, do they have to prepare an EIS?" Breyer asked, acknowledging that he was being somewhat facetious.

"No," Kendall replied, adding that NRDC has never suggested that any of the precautions it wants the Navy to take should apply to combat. Instead, the case is all about making sure that whales and other marine mammals don't have to die while the Navy is practicing.

The hourlong hearing covered a lot of ground. Both sides appearing before the court get 30 minutes to make their case and answer the justices' questions—which started flying within the first couple of minutes of both lawyers' prepared arguments.

Speaking for the Navy, Solicitor General Gregory Garre disputed whether a large number of marine mammals would suffer long-term harm as a result of the sonar exercises. He repeated the phrase "non-injurious, temporary exposures" over and over when Justices Samuel Alito and Ruth Bader Ginsburg tried to nail him down.

But Kendall said the factual assertions the Navy has made about the harm to whales are completely disproven by the military's own environmental assessment scientists. The evidence that sonar has caused beaked whale strandings around the world—with the whales washed up on beaches bleeding from the ears and brain—is overwhelmingly supported by scientific studies, Kendall said. He asked the justices to imagine the noise of a jet engine multiplied by 2,000 times filling the courtroom. That's the same impact that a sonar blast can have on whales, dolphins and other marine mammals, Kendall said.

Who Won the Oral Argument?

Here's what I'm sure you really want to know: Does it look like the Navy or NRDC won today? My answer: I haven't got a clue. And I doubt that anyone else does, either.

"I've been doing this a long time, and I've given up reading the tea leaves," Kendall said outside the courtroom after arguing on NRDC's behalf.

The justices had a lot of tough questions for both sides, which is what you would expect in a Supreme Court case. If it were an easy call, why would it wind up in the highest court in the land?

Kendall said the questions are often designed to ferret out what the lawyers are thinking about the case, and tough queries don't necessarily indicate that a justice disagrees with one position or another. Still, it seemed pretty clear that at least Justice Antonin Scalia has the Navy's back, because he appeared to be assisting the solicitor general with his arguments at a couple of points.

And Justice David Souter appeared to be taking NRDC's side, saying the national emergency that the White House declared to exempt the Navy from environmental laws was in fact "created by the failure of the Navy" to do the proper environmental impact study.

I checked a few news outlets that employ seasoned Supreme Court reporters to see how they're reading the case. The *Los Angeles Times* said the "justices sounded closely split today on whether environmental laws can be used to protect whales and other marine mammals from the Navy's use of sonar off the coast of Southern California," and the Associated Press also said that the court "appeared divided." The *New York Times* leads off with the justices who "indicated an inclination to overturn" the lower court's decision protecting whales.

Arguing before the Supreme Court isn't like a presidential debate. If the lawyers don't answer the questions they're asked, or if they try to change the subject, the justices just keep coming back at them. (Of the court's nine justices, only Clarence Thomas didn't ask anything this morning.)

You could tell that both Kendall and Garre had a lot of points they were hoping to make today. But the solicitor general, who argued first, didn't even make it a minute into his argument before Justice Ginsburg cut in with the first question. Kendall had even less time when his half hour came.

Here are some of the main points that the justices kept bringing up (and how the attorneys dealt with them):

Sonar's Impact on Whales

Ginsburg's initial question concerned the details of the injunction issued by the lower courts to prevent the naval exercises from harming whales. Then Justice Alito jumped in with the second query, asking Garre about the number of marine mammals likely to be killed or injured by sonar blasts—as opposed to simply "disrupted."

"No marine mammal would be killed as a result of these exercises," Garre declared, citing several times the Navy's "293-page" environmental assessment. A handful of animals—dolphins, not whales—could suffer permanent injuries, he said, but the vast majority would suffer only temporary disruptions.

"In lay terms, what does that mean?" Alito asked. Garre said: "There's a learning response. They hear the sound and they go in the opposite direction."

When Kendall got his chance later, he said the Navy's own studies—as well as scientists around the world—show that just isn't true. He talked about necropsies [scientific examinations of dead animals] of beaked whales whose bodies have been found on beaches, which show hemorrhaging and embolisms from the impact of sonar.

Garre asserted that the Navy has been conducting exercises off California for 40 years with no evidence of mass strandings. There's a simple reason for that, Kendall said later: No one was looking. "Until very recently," he elaborated to reporters after the hearing, "no one was studying the effects of sonar at all." Now that scientists are aware of the problem, the evidence for it is overwhelming.

What Gives Them the Right?

The outcome of this case may hinge on whether the White House has the authority to grant the Navy an exemption from the National Environmental Policy Act, which it did after a lower court imposed additional safeguards on naval training exercises. (An office of the White House called the Council on Environmental Quality [CEQ] actually issued the ruling.)

Justice Souter wanted to know where in the statute it says that the CEQ can exempt a government agency from preparing an environmental impact statement. "I want to know what the statutory authority is," he repeated several times.

Chief Justice John Roberts followed on that same line by asking why the Navy went to CEQ, which isn't mentioned in NEPA. "It seems to me that CEQ is an odd body to be doing this, as an arm of the White House," Roberts said.

Garre said the government's position is that the Navy complied with the requirements of NEPA by complying with the alternative requirements created by the CEQ.

After the hearing, Kendall told reporters why it's so important that the White House not be allowed to let the Navy ignore NEPA's requirements. The act says government agencies are supposed to study the ways that they can avoid harming the environment before taking action, Kendall said. The Navy didn't do that here.

"If they can blow a hole through NEPA," Kendall said, "that would affect our lives in so many ways."

Litigation Was Necessary

Breyer—who got pretty much all of the morning's best lines—said at one point that he's no expert in naval warfare or marine mammals, and that neither are the lower court judges who previously ruled in the case.

"Why couldn't you work this thing out?" he asked, rather than forcing the courts to resolve the conflicting evidence over whether sonar harms whales and what protections are good enough.

"The Navy is focused on having its own way or no way," Kendall responded, provoking a, "That's not fair," from Chief Justice Roberts. He said the Navy had already taken its own steps to protect marine mammals. But Kendall said they're too weak.

"We negotiated with the Navy for months and months and months," he said. Only the threat of litigation, and the court rulings in NRDC's favor, will force the military to make the changes that are needed, Kendall added.

"They wanted the blank check they're asking for here today," Kendall told reporters later, "and we simply cannot go that far."

"Hopefully, the court will set aside the
long-held notion within the federal judiciary that the Endangered Species Act
is a super statute that trumps all other
public considerations."

Environmental Laws Should Not Be Allowed to Thwart Defense Preparedness

David Stirling

*David Stirling is vice president of the Pacific Legal Foundation,
which filed a Supreme Court brief in* Winter v. NRDC. *He is
the author of* Green Gone Wild—Elevating Nature Above Human Rights. *In the following commentary written before the Supreme Court reached its decision in* Winter v. Natural Resources
Defense Council, *he argues that environmental protection laws
should not override all other socially beneficial public interests,
and that restricting the use of sonar in Navy training exercises to
avoid harming whales would hurt national security. The idea
that endangered species must be protected "whatever the cost"
originated with the 1978 case* TVA v. Hill, *he says, and in his
opinion this interpretation is a misunderstanding of the Endangered Species Act. It has been applied in many cases where it has
resulted in harm to the public, and abandoning it would allow
the courts to return to their traditional role of weighing and balancing competing benefits.*

David Stirling, "Security vs. Species Preservation," *Washington Times*, October 5, 2008.
Reproduced by permission.

This Wednesday [October 8, 2008], the U.S. Supreme Court will hear a case that could define how we approach national security.

Whatever one thinks of the war on terror or U.S. military activities in Iraq and Afghanistan, most Americans feel strongly that our men and women in uniform should have the most advanced equipment, weaponry and protective gear and be thoroughly prepared through training and practice to protect our national security.

Environmentalist organizations, on the other hand, believe federal environmental laws trump national security and the American military personnel who provide it.

That's why they filed a lawsuit against the U.S. Navy to stop its sonar training exercises off the coast of Southern California. Why? Because they claim marine mammals like the beaked whale—listed as "threatened" under the Endangered Species Act—were harmed when the sonar waves move through the ocean.

But for more than 40 years, the Navy has conducted training exercises with mid-frequency active (MFA) sonar and no incidents of harm or large-scale whale-beachings attributable to the exercises have been recorded. The Navy even recently issued a lengthy environmental assessment stating there were no documented incidents of harm, injury or death to marine mammals resulting from exposure to sonar in the Southern California training area.

What's more, the National Marine Fisheries Service, the federal agency responsible for protecting and preserving marine mammals under the Endangered Species Act and related statutes, issued a Biological Opinion concluding that the Navy's use of sonar was not likely to jeopardize the continued existence of any listed species.

Nevertheless, a federal district court restricted the Navy's use of sonar so severely as to negate the training value of the exercise. But this will only serve to hurt our national security efforts.

With the quiet-running diesel-electric submarines used by erratic and unfriendly nations operating in the western Pacific and Middle East, the Navy regards its training exercises as the only effective means to prepare its strike groups to detect submarines before they close within weapons range.

The Navy believes restrictions on the use of sonar impose unacceptable risks to the timely deployment of strike groups to the Middle East and to national security. And the president [George W. Bush] issued an exemption to "enable the Navy to train effectively and to certify . . . strike groups for deployment" in support of operational and combat activities "essential to national security."

Despite these clear statements of the importance of the sonar training exercises, the U.S. 9th Circuit Court of Appeals upheld the district court's restrictions on the use of sonar, declaring, "The armed forces must take precautionary measures to comply with the [environmental] law during its training."

It's this elevation of the environmental laws to thwart national security preparedness that caused the Supreme Court to take up the case, *Natural Resources Defense Council v. Donald C. Winter, Secretary of the Navy.*

Hopefully, the court will set aside the long-held notion within the federal judiciary that the Endangered Species Act is a super statute that trumps all other public considerations. This faulty line of thinking got its start in the 1978 Supreme Court decision in *TVA v. Hill* (the snail darter case) where it declared Congress intended the ESA to preserve plant and wildlife species "whatever the cost."

Since the court's unfortunate use of that imperious phrase, federal district and appellate courts have regularly elevated species preservation above all other socially beneficial public interests.

Some of the better-known examples of this disturbing trend include: drilling halted for domestic sources of oil and natural gas because of listed species; timber harvests stopped in the name of the northern spotted owl, causing overgrown forests to be threatened by catastrophic wildfire; shutting off passage of river water to households and farmers during drought conditions for the benefit of fish; stopping construction of hurricane barrier gates out of concern for shrimp and shell fish—gates that would have protected New Orleans from Katrina's deadly storm surge.

In deciding *Winter v. NRDC,* the Supreme Court could do the country a great and long overdue service by correcting the general misunderstanding of the ESA's species-preservation bias that followed the court's language—"whatever the cost." Removal of that mandate would restore to trial court judges their traditional role of weighing and balancing the equities between species preservation and competing economic and social public benefits.

Of course, litigious environmentalist organizations like those that filed the suit would vehemently oppose such a reasonable outcome, so holding one's breath is not recommended.

"*The overriding lesson of* Winter v. NRDC *is that our legal system is ill-equipped to protect the natural world.*"

The U.S. Legal System Is Ill Equipped to Protect the Natural World

Mary Munson

Mary Munson is legal director of the Center for Earth Jurisprudence at the Law Schools of Barry and St. Thomas universities. In the following commentary she argues that the Supreme Court's decision in Winter v. Natural Resources Defense Council, *which favored naval training over the welfare of marine mammals, shows that the U.S. legal system cannot protect nature and needs to be redesigned. In the first place, she says, animals should be given legal standing. In the second place, environmental laws should be strengthened. And in the third place, the legal system should recognize that ecological balance rests on the interdependence of all species. In Munson's opinion, the fundamental question about how conflicts between humans and nature are resolved should depend not on politics, but on a system of respect for nonhumans as well as humans.*

On Nov. 12, [2008,] the Supreme Court ruled in favor of the Navy's right to use sonar that can be fatal to dolphins, whales and other marine mammals.

The case was a challenge to the use of high-intensity sonar in the Navy's submarine detection training exercises. The

Natural Resources Defense Council (NRDC) and its co-plaintiffs claimed that the exercises harmed marine mammals by causing bleeding, lesions and disorientation. A lower court agreed and imposed six restrictions on the exercises.

This Supreme Court case was an appeal of two of those restrictions: shutting down the sonar when a marine mammal was spotted, and powering down under other circumstances near the surface. Using the laws and legal doctrines at hand, Chief Justice John Roberts easily dismissed the interests of the whales and dolphins and overturned those restrictions. He said he must defer to the Navy's judgment that the restrictions would compromise its ability to defend national security.

The setback could have been worse, since the Navy challenged only two of the six restrictions. But it showed that the Supreme Court is less disposed to protecting nature than [are] the lower courts. And more important, the case exposed some fundamental difficulties in protecting nature in the face of a court with that predisposition.

Laws Have Failed to Protect Nature

The overriding lesson of *Winter v. NRDC* is that our legal system is ill-equipped to protect the natural world. This may already be evident since we are beset with global warming and mass extinctions. But the case exposes some practical ways our laws need improvement. The problems center around the way courts define the "public interest" to apply only to "human" interests. Our system does not recognize that the Earth is a web of interrelated, interdependent beings, and natural systems need to function together so all species can flourish. In this case, laws failed nature in three ways.

- First, in our legal system, animals do not have standing in court. NRDC could not argue on behalf of the marine creatures themselves. It could argue only that NRDC itself would be harmed if the sea creatures could not be watched or photographed. This affected

the outcome in favor of the Navy. We need to change
our laws so that life other than human life can be represented legally.

- Second, our environmental laws themselves are weak.
  Marine mammal and coastal zone protection laws have
  exemptions for military maneuvers so when it goes
  back to the lower courts, much of the case relies on the
  National Environmental Policy Act. NEPA requires
  agencies only to assess environmental impacts before
  taking actions. So even if the NEPA claim is won, sonar
  can be used once the studies are performed (even if the
  studies conclude that the tests are harmful). To protect
  nature, laws must be strengthened.

- Finally, our laws treat this problem as if it is a U.S.
  problem alone, not one that concerns other countries'
  relationships to the environment and marine creatures.
  It exposes how U.S. domestic laws only weakly enforce
  the few international environmental agreements in
  which we participate. To promote environmental protection, the United States must become a stronger international player.

We need to redesign our legal system to recognize that
ecological balance rests on the interdependence of all species,
humans as well as dolphins. *Winter v. NRDC* involved a preliminary injunction, so the questions will continue to be
played out in courts. . . . The fundamental question about
how conflicts between humans and nature are resolved must
not depend on politics and appointees to courts; it must be
addressed through a new system that values and respects the
nonhuman sphere as well as the human one.

> *"As the judges see it, national defense is not the precondition of every legal safeguard, but just one consideration to balance among many others."*

Winter Could Alter the Balance Between Environmental Concerns and National Defense

Jeremy Rabkin

Jeremy Rabkin is a professor of law at George Mason University in Arlington, Virginia. In the following viewpoint, he argues that what is most notable about the Supreme Court's decision in Winter v. Natural Resources Defense Council *is how narrow it was. Although the navy won the case, only five of the nine justices signed the majority opinion, and in order to get that majority, the opinion had to emphasize that military interests are not always an overriding factor. In the past, it has been taken for granted that national defense outweighs other considerations. Now, although animal welfare activists say they do not advocate restricting naval operations for the sake of whales in actual combat situations, some environmental laws do not explicitly exempt such situations. The navy, contends Rabkin, made a strong case for its assertion that training missions are essential preparation for combat. He is dismayed by the fact that in going to war, Americans knowingly take action in which tens of thousands of*

Jeremy Rabkin, "Winter Case Spells Cold Climate For Military In the Courts," Human Events.com, November 17, 2008. Reproduced by permission.

human beings will die, yet the Supreme Court now appears
ready to balance national defense against action that risks harm
to hundreds of marine mammals.

During oral argument [in October 2008], Justice Stephen Breyer put this question: "You go on a bombing mission—do you have to prepare an environmental impact statement?"

Los Angeles lawyer Richard Kendall, representing the Natural Resources Defense Council, was the man responsible for answering. In *Winter v. NRDC*, environmental advocates were urging the Supreme Court to uphold the orders of federal courts in California (against Navy Secretary Winter) which would have sharply constrained planned navy training exercises off the Pacific coast. NRDC had persuaded west coast judges that the sonar equipment to be used by the navy might injure whales and dolphins and so should be restrained until the navy completed a full scale environmental impact statement, assessing the relevant risks.

So Breyer's question was quite pertinent. If courts could restrain training exercises, why not actual combat missions? Kendall's answer was straight-forward: "No, of course not in combat. But here in a training exercise, the military is supposed to minimize the damage."

But the underlying statute, the National Environmental Policy Act [NEPA] of 1969, makes no explicit exception for combat operations. It calls for federal agencies to prepare an environmental impact statement for any "major Federal action significantly affecting the quality of the human environment," cautioning only that this obligation should be honored "to the fullest extent possible."

The Marine Mammal Protection Act of 1972, which might have been relevant as well in this case, includes an explicit authorization for the Secretary of Defense to exempt from its prohibitions "any action or category of actions . . . necessary for national defense." Was it any stretch to assume that NEPA should be read to authorize something similar?

The navy certainly made strong arguments for the importance to "national defense" of the particular sonar training involved here. Sonar operators need practice in order to track the position and direction of enemy submarines, but the navy also needs to practice coordinating information and responses with other ships in a "strike group" (usually organized around an aircraft carrier). The navy wanted to give such groups practice in joint operations off the California coast before setting off to more hostile waters in the Middle East.

A Narrow Decision

The navy won the case—at least in the form it was put to the Supreme Court. But what's most notable about the Court's decision in *Winter v. NRDC* is how very narrow and cautious it is. Only five justices signed on to the majority opinion by Chief Justice Roberts, which emphasized the rather technical point that the lower courts should have reconsidered their claims, given the navy's willingness to adhere to four of the six restrictions originally imposed by the district court.

So far from urging general deference to military considerations, the majority opinion took pains to emphasize that environmental claims might triumph in the next case: "Of course, military interests do not always trump other considerations and we have not held that they do."

The Pentagon certainly does devote a great deal of effort to assessing (and then trying to ameliorate) environmental harms that might result from all its construction projects, its far-flung bases and ports and transport systems. Even in this case, the navy had promised to produce a full environmental impact statement for future training exercises with sonar and had already undertaken a streamlined "environmental assessment" to reassure critics that the dangers to marine mammals were not excessive.

So you might think there would be a lot of case law on how to balance environmental priorities with military needs. But *Winter* cites no case on point. No case of this kind has reached the Supreme Court, and the handful of cases in lower courts have questioned the siting of bases, rather than asking courts to review precise military practices in combat-simulating exercises.

What *Winter* really suggests, therefore, is that old assumptions about deference are fading. The dissent by Justices [Ruth Bader] Ginsburg and [David] Souter protests that if the navy needed an exemption, it should have asked Congress to enact such a measure rather than seeking—as it did—guidance from "an executive council" (the White House Council on Environmental Quality, which approved the navy's proposed training exercises with some slight modifications to reduce environmental risks). The dissenters seem to question (as a number of commentators have) that the balance between environmental and defense priorities should be struck by officials answering to the president, as if the president's responsibilities as commander-in-chief somehow disqualify him from balancing security with other concerns.

Justices Breyer and [John Paul] Stevens explained, in their concurring opinion, that they would normally have asked lower courts to consider fashioning a more accommodating injunction, except that the navy's plans for December training exercises did not leave time for that. The conservative justices could only get five votes by affirming their willingness to consider an environmental injunction against the military in some future case.

But here's the thing. When we go to war, we knowingly undertake actions in which human beings will die, as tens of thousands of human beings have already been killed in Iraq since our invasion in 2003. Courts aren't yet willing to second-guess combat decisions, despite the human stakes. But the Supreme Court has now indicated that it may be ready to second-guess essential preparation for combat, if military policy risks harm (as environmental advocates claimed here) to hundreds of marine mammals.

As the judges see it, national defense is not the precondition of every legal safeguard, but just one consideration to balance among many others. And the judges trust themselves to strike the final balance.

Organizations to Contact

The editors have compiled the following list of organizations concerned with the issues debated in this book. The descriptions are derived from materials provided by the organizations. All have publications or information available for interested readers. The list was compiled on the date of publication of the present volume; the information provided here may change. Be aware that many organizations take several weeks or longer to respond to inquiries, so allow as much time as possible.

American Cetacean Society
PO Box 1391, San Pedro, CA   90733
(310) 548-6279
Web site: www.acsonline.org

The American Cetacean Society is a nonprofit organization that protects whales, dolphins, porpoises, and their habitats through public education, research grants, and conservation actions. Its Web site contains extensive educational information about marine mammals and issues involving them.

**American Society for the Prevention of Cruelty
to Animals (ASPCA)**
424 E. Ninety-Second Street, New York, NY   10128-6804
(212) 876-7700
e-mail: education@aspca.org
www.aspca.org

The American Society for the Prevention of Cruelty to Animals was the first humane society established in America and is one of the largest in the world. Its mission is to provide effective means for the prevention of cruelty to animals throughout the United States, and it is dedicated to fulfilling this mission through nonviolent approaches. Its Web site contains policy and position statements on many issues concerning the welfare of animals.

American Veterinary Medical Association (AVMA)
1931 N. Meacham Road, Suite 100, Schaumburg, IL 60173
(800) 248-2862 • fax: (847) 925-1329
e-mail: avmainfo@avma.org
Web site: www.avma.org

The American Veterinary Medical Association is a major non-profit association of veterinarians. Its mission is to improve animal and human health and advance the veterinary medical profession. Its Web site contains detailed discussions of animal welfare, including policy statements and background information on farm practices that have been criticized.

Americans for Medical Progress (AMP)
526 King Street, Suite 201, Alexandria, VA 22314
(703) 836-9595 • fax: (703) 836-9594
e-mail: info@amprogress.org
Web site: www.amprogress.org

Americans for Medical Progress is a nonprofit organization whose purpose is to nurture public understanding of and support for the humane, necessary, and valuable use of animals in medicine. It argues that threats by animal rights extremists hurt medical progress. Its Web site contains facts about animal research, information about violent tactics used by animal rights groups, and personal stories of people who have been helped by medical advances obtained through animal research.

Animal Legal Defense Fund (ALDF)
170 E. Cotati Ave., Cotati, CA 94931
(707) 795-2533 • fax: (707) 795-7280
e-mail: info@www.aldf.org
Web site: www.aldf.org

The Animal Legal Defense Fund fights to protect the lives and advance the interests of animals through the legal system. It files lawsuits, provides free legal assistance to prosecutors handling cruelty cases, and works to strengthen anticruelty laws. Its Web site contains information about cases in which it has been involved.

Animal Legal & Historical Web Center
Michigan State University College of Law
East Lansing, MI 48824-1300
e-mail: editor@animallaw.info
Web site: www.animallaw.info

This university-operated site contains information about past and present court cases involving animals plus explanations of some of the more interesting issues of animal law in addition to legal articles addressing a wide variety of animal topics.

Animal Welfare Information Center (AWIC)
National Agricultural Library, Beltsville, MD 20705
(301) 504-6212 • fax: (301) 504-7125
e-mail: awic@ars.usda.gov
Web site: http://awic.nal.usda.gov

Animal Welfare Information Center is operated by the U.S. Department of Agriculture as mandated by the Animal Welfare Act to provide information for improved animal care and use in research, testing, teaching, and exhibition. Its Web site provides information on methods and sources available to reduce, refine, or replace animals used for these purposes, as well as general information about animal use.

Center for Consumer Freedom
PO Box 34557, Washington, DC 20043
(202) 463-7112
Web site: www.consumerfreedom.com

The Center for Consumer Freedom is a nonprofit organization devoted to promoting personal responsibility and protecting consumer choices. It opposes all forms of activism, including animal rights activism, that aim to restrict the individual choices of consumers. Among other projects, it supports the sites Animal Scam (www.animalscam.com) and PETA Kills Animals (petakillsanimals.com), which expose what the center terms the extremist views and hypocritical actions of radical animal-rights organizations.

Defenders of Wildlife

1130 Seventeenth Street NW, Washington, DC   20036

(800) 385-9712

Web site: www.defenders.org

The Defenders of Wildlife is a large nonprofit organization that works to protect and restore America's native wildlife, safeguard wildlife habitat, and resolve conflicts. It works across international borders to educate and mobilize the public. Its Web site contains detailed information, including some videos, about many endangered species of animals.

Farm Sanctuary

PO Box 150, Watkins Glen, NY   14891

(607) 583-2225 ext. 221

e-mail: info@farmsanctuary.org

Web site: www.farmsanctuary.org

Farm Sanctuary is a nonprofit organization that works to prevent cruelty to animals and to encourage legal and policy reforms that promote respect and compassion for farm animals. It advocates veganism. Its Web site contains information about its policies and activities plus downloadable educational materials titled *Cultivating Compassion: Teachers' Guide and Student Activities.*

Fur Commission USA (FCUSA)

826 Orange Ave., Coronado, CA   92118-2698

(619) 575-0139 • fax: (619) 575-5578

e-mail: furfarmers@aol.com

Fur Commission USA is an agricultural association representing fur farmers. In addition to information about fur farming, its Web Site contains material about the difference between the animal welfare movement and the animal rights movement, including many quotations from spokespeople for both.

Humane Society of the United States (HSUS)
2100 L Street NW, Washington, DC 20037
(202) 452-1100
Web site: www.hsus.org

Humane Society of the United States is the nation's largest animal protection organization. It works to reduce animals' suffering and to create meaningful social change for animals by advocating for sensible public policies, investigating cruelty and working to enforce existing laws, and educating the public about animal issues. It publishes *All Animals*, a membership magazine, and *Animal Sheltering*, a bimonthly magazine for animal sheltering professionals. Its Web site contains detailed information about cruelty to animals.

International Primate Protection League (IPPL)
PO Box 766, Summerville, SC 29484
(843) 871-2280 • fax: (843) 871-7988
e-mail: info@ippl.org
Web site: www.ippl.org

International Primate Protection League is a nonprofit organization dedicated to protecting the world's remaining primates. It offers support for activities that help monkeys and apes, publicizes the plight of primates in trouble, organizes international protest campaigns, and conducts investigations of illegal international primate trafficking. Its Web site contains information about its accomplishments and all its archived newsletters, including periodic updates about the Silver Spring monkeys.

Natural Resources Defense Council (NRDC)
40 W. Twentieth Street, New York, NY 10011
(212) 727-2700 • fax: (212) 727-1773
e-mail: nrdcinfo@nrdc.org
Web site: www.nrdc.org

The Natural Resources Defense Council is one of the nation's most powerful environmental groups. It is a nonprofit organization that aims to safeguard the earth: its people, its plants and animals, and the natural systems on which all life depends. Its Web site contains extensive information on all areas of environmentalism, including a section on endangered wildlife and its court action to protect whales from military sonar.

People for the Ethical Treatment of Animals (PETA)
501 Front Street, Norfolk, VA   23510
(757) 622-7382 • fax: (757) 622-0457
Web site: www.peta.org

People for the Ethical Treatment of Animals is a large activist organization that advocates for animal rights. It opposes the use of animals by humans for any purpose whatsoever: for food, clothing, research, or entertainment. Its Web site contains material about the mistreatment of animals as well as information about supporting the animal rights movement.

For Further Research

Books

Susan Armstrong, *The Animal Ethics Reader*. New York: Routledge, 2008.

Tom L. Beauchamp et al., *The Human Use of Animals: Case Studies in Ethical Choice*. New York: Oxford University Press, 2008.

Diane L. Beers, *For the Prevention of Cruelty: The History and Legacy of Animal Rights Activism in the United States*. Athens, OH: Swallow Press/Ohio University Press, 2006.

Marc Bekoff, *Animals Matter: A Biologist Explains Why We Should Treat Animals with Compassion and Respect*. Boston: Shambhala, 2007.

———, ed., *Encyclopedia of Animal Rights and Animal Welfare*. Santa Barbara, CA: Greenwood/ABC-CLIO, 2009.

Linda Birke, Arnold Arluke, and Mike Michael, *The Sacrifice: How Scientific Experiments Transform Animals and People*. West Lafayette, IN: Purdue University Press, 2007.

Deborah Blum, *The Monkey Wars*. New York: Oxford University Press, 1994.

Karen Dawn, *Thanking the Monkey: Rethinking the Way We Treat Animals*. New York: HarperCollins, 2008.

Gail A. Eisnitz, *Slaughterhouse: The Shocking Story of Greed, Neglect, and Inhumane Treatment Inside the U.S. Meat Industry*. Amherst, NY: Prometheus Books, 2007.

David S. Favre, *Animal Law: Welfare, Interests, and Rights*. New York: Aspen, 2008.

Gary L. Francione, *Animals as Persons: Essays on the Abolition of Animal Exploitation.* New York: Columbia University Press, 2008.

David Fraser, *Understanding Animal Welfare: The Science in Its Cultural Context.* Ames, IA: Wiley-Blackwell, 2008.

Temple Grandin and Catherine Johnson, *Animals Make Us Human: Creating the Best Life for Animals.* Boston: Houghton Mifflin Harcourt, 2009.

Mark Hawthorne, *Striking at the Roots: A Practical Guide to Animal Activism.* Washington, DC: O Books, 2008.

Erik Marcus, *Meat Market: Animals, Ethics, and Money.* Boston: Brio, 2005.

Adrian R. Morrison, *An Odyssey with Animals: A Veterinarian's Reflections on the Animal Rights and Welfare Debate.* New York: Oxford University Press, 2009.

Alex Pacheco and Anna Francione, "The Silver Spring Monkeys," in *In Defense of Animals.* Ed. Peter Singer. New York: Perennial Library, 1986.

Clive Phillips, *The Welfare of Animals: The Silent Majority.* New York: Springer, 2008.

Peter Sandøe and Stine B. Christiansen, *Ethics of Animal Use.* Ames, IA: Wiley-Blackwell, 2008.

Jeffrey M. Schwartz and Sharon Begley, "The Silver Springs Monkeys," in *The Mind and the Brain: Neuroplasticity and the Power of Mental Force.* New York: Harper-Collins, 2002.

Kathryn Shevelow, *For the Love of Animals: The Rise of the Animal Protection Movement.* New York: Henry Holt, 2008.

Peter Singer, ed., *In Defense of Animals: The Second Wave.* Malden, MA: Blackwell, 2006.

Cass R. Sunstein and Martha C. Nussbaum, eds., *Animal Rights: Current Debates and New Directions*. New York: Oxford University Press, 2004.

Bob Torres, *Making a Killing: The Political Economy of Animal Rights*. Oakland, CA: AK Press, 2007.

Erin E. Williams and Margo Demello, *Why Animals Matter: The Case for Animal Protection*. Amherst, NY: Prometheus Books, 2007.

Periodicals

Bonnie Azab-Powell, "This Little Piggy Goes Home," *Mother Jones*, March/April 2009.

Kate Blake, "Animal Welfare," *America*, March 23, 2009.

Sholto Byrnes, "Using Animals for Research Is More Justifiable than Eating Them for Pleasure," *New Statesman*, March 3, 2008.

Jon Cohen, "Humane Society Launches Offensive to Ban Invasive Chimp Research," *Science*, March 13, 2009.

P. Michael Conn and James V. Parker, "Winners and Losers in the Animal-Research War," *American Scientist*, May/June 2008.

Current Events, "Do Animals Have Rights?" April 27, 2009.

Russell Dick, "Collateral Damage," *Mother Jones*, March/April 2006.

Kate Douglas, "Just Like Us," *New Scientist*, June 2, 2007.

Caroline Fraser, "The Raid at Silver Spring," *New Yorker*, April 19, 1993.

Bridget Goldschmidt, "A Kinder, Gentler," *Progressive Grocer*, December 2008.

Good Medicine "Replacing Animals in Medical Education," Spring 2008.

Kendall Hemphill, "Shooting the Groundhog," *Texas Fish & Game*, May 2008.

Becky McKay Johnson, "Farm Sanctuary," *Journal of Agricultural & Food Information*, January 2009.

Jean Johnson, "Opening the Cages," *E—the Environmental Magazine*, July/August 2007.

Josh Keller, "For Researchers on Animals, Ethics Training Is Sparse," *Chronicle of Higher Education*, September 19, 2008.

Warren E. Leary, "Renewal of Brain Is Found in Disputed Monkey Tests," *New York Times*, June 28, 1991.

Adam Liptak, "Court Weighs Concerns on Whales and Military," *New York Times*, October 8, 2008.

———, "Environmental Groups Find Less Support from Justices," *New York Times*, July 4, 2009.

———, "Supreme Court Rules for Navy in Sonar Case," *New York Times*, November 13, 2008.

Meg Major, "Handle with Care," *Progressive Grocer*, April 1, 2007.

Lori Marino, "Another Kind of Scientist Activism," *Chronicle of Higher Education*, March 30, 2009.

Jesse McKinley, "White House Exempts Navy from Sonar Ban, Angering Environmental Groups," *New York Times*, January 17, 2008.

Jeff McMahon, "Eating Animals the Nice Way," *Daedalus*, Winter 2008.

Donald G. McNeil, "The Inalienable Rights of Apes?" *New York Times Upfront*, October 6, 2008.

Peter Monaghan, "The Growing Field of Animal Law Is Attracting Activists and Pragmatists Alike," *Chronicle of Higher Education*, June 29, 2007.

Jim Motavalli, "Rights from Wrongs: A Movement to Grant Legal Protection to Animals Is Gathering Force," *E—the Environmental Magazine*, March/April 2003.

George Pelecanos, "Barking Mad," *New Republic*, September 10, 2007.

Seth Perry, "Lives in the Balance," *Chronicle of Higher Education*, January 26, 2007.

Robert Reinhold, "Fate of Monkeys, Deformed for Science, Causes Human Hurt After 6 Years," *New York Times*, May 23, 1987.

Wesley J. Smith, "Four Legs Good, Two Legs Bad: The Anti-Human Values of 'Animal Rights,'" *Human Life Review*, Winter 2007.

———, "Monkey Business," *Weekly Standard*, July 21, 2008.

David Stout, "Suit Challenges Image of Circus Elephants as Willing Performers," *New York Times*, January 31, 2009.

Jennifer Weeks, "Factory Farms," *CQ Researcher*, January 12, 2007.

Karin Winegar and Regan Dunnick, "The Slaughter Debate," *Horse & Rider*, November 2007.

Daniel Zwerdling, "A View to a Kill," *Gourmet*, June 2007.

Internet Sources

Peter Singer and Bruce Friedrich, "Promoting Animal Rights by Promoting Reform," *Animals Australia*, 2007. www.animalsaustralia.org.

Index

A

Administrative Procedure Act
(APA), 60, 81
Administrators of the Tulane Education Fund, 26
Aesthetic injury, 83, 85–87
Agricultural law, 134
Agricultural practices. *See* Routine husbandry practices
Alito, Samuel, 165
Allen v. Wright (1984), 28
American Society for the Prevention of Cruelty to Animals v. Ringling Brothers and Barnum & Bailey Circus (2003), 85, 86–87
American Veterinary Medical Association (AVMA), 102, 107
Americans United for Separation of Church and State, Valley Forge Christian College v. (1982), 31, 34
Amoco Production Co. v. Gambell (1987), 148
Anderson, Pamela, 66
Animal abuse, by owners, 40–42
Animal law, 134
Animal Legal Defense Fund v. Glickman (1998), 85–88
Animal Legal Defense Fund v. Veneman (2007), 85, 86
Animal Liberation (Singer), 15
Animal owners, as abusers, 40–42
Animal rights activists
   on farm animals, 91
   image of, 122

inflammatory statements by, 15
Animal rights movement
   aims of, 52
   vs. animal welfare movement, 14–16, 128–135
   campaigns by, 122–127
   civil rights movement and, 76
Animal Welfare Act (AWA)
   Department of Agriculture and, 85
   enforcement of, 39, 40
   purpose of, 39, 42, 71–72
   rules for medical research in, 16
   suits filed under, 38
Animal welfare advocates
   lack standing, 29–35
   right of, to choose court to sue in, 25–28
Animal Welfare Institute, 121
Animal welfare laws
   on farm animals, 92, 94
   purpose of, 42
   support for, 16
Animal welfare movement
   vs. animal rights movement, 14–16, 128–135
   on farm animal treatment, 92, 120–127
   growth of, 121–127
Animal welfare, public interest in, 14–15
Animals
   are more than personal property, 36–45
   circus, 17–18, 85
   in court, 83–85

New Jersey Society for the Prevention of Cruelty to Animals et al. v. New Jersey Department of Agriculture (2008)
  appellants' brief in, 106–118
  case overview, 91–92
  court's opinion in, 93–105
  debate over humane farming practices and, 128–135
Newkirk, Ingrid, 15
Niman Ranch Pork Company, 132

O

Oil drilling, 169–170
O'Leary, Denyse, 46–50
O'Neill, Sausalito v. (2004), 59

P

Pacelle, Wayne, 123–124
Pacheco, Alex, 20–21, 38
Palila v. Hawaii Department of Land and Natural Resources (1986), 44, 57–58, 84
Patrick, Sharon, 124
People for the Ethical Treatment of Animals (PETA)
  advertising campaign by, 15
  campaigns by, 123
  establishment of, 20
  image of, 122
  on medical research, 49
  Silver Spring monkeys and, 20–24
Perry Lang, Adam, 126
Personal property, animals are more than, 36–45
Pigs
  confinement of, 110–111, 131

humanely raised, 132
ringing of, 131
Polacheck, Lori, 69–70
Poultry practices, 103, 112–113, 117
Primate Protection League v. Tulane Educational Fund (1991)
  brief for NIH in, 29–35
  case overview, 20–24
  unanimous opinion in, 25–28
Public interest, 172
Puck, Wolfgang, 124

R

Rabkin, Jeremy, 174–178
Rainbow Friends Animal Sanctuary, 52
Rattling the Cage (Wise), 74
Rights
  legal, of animals, 59, 71–74, 83, 87–88
  statutory *vs.* guaranteed, 71–72
Ringling Brothers and Barnum & Bailey Circus, 17–18
Ringling Brothers and Barnum & Bailey Circus, American Society for the Prevention of Cruelty to Animals v. (2003), 85, 86–87
Roberts, John, 140–152, 165, 166, 172, 176
Rollin, Bernard, 99
Roosevelt, Theodore, 152
Routine husbandry practices
  authorization of, 98–101
  cruelty of, 106–118
  debate over, 128–135
  definition of, 95–96, 99–101, 115

dissenting opinion in, 153–160

majority opinion in, 140–152

oral arguments in, 161–166

Wise, Steven, 74, 75–76

Wright, Allen v. (1984), 26

Z

Zoos, 17, 21, 82, 85–86